CHASING LIFE

BRANDT LEGG

By Brandt Legg

Chase Malone Thriller

Chasing Rain
Chasing Fire
Chasing Wind
Chasing Dirt
Chasing Life
Chasing Kill
Chasing Risk
Chasing Mind
Chasing Time
Chasing Lies
Chasing Fear
Chasing Lost

As always, this book is dedicated to
Teakki and Ro

Vinci Books

vinci-books.com

Published by Vinci Books Ltd in 2025

1

Copyright © Brandt Legg 2020

The author has asserted their moral right to be identified as the author of this work in accordance with the Copyright, Designs and Patents Act 1988. This work is a work of fiction. Names, characters, places and incidents are the product of the author's imagination or are used fictitiously. Any resemblance to actual persons, living or dead, places and incidents is entirely coincidental.

All rights reserved. No part of this publication may be copied, reproduced, distributed, stored in any retrieval system, or transmitted in any form or by any means, including photocopying, recording, or other electronic or mechanical methods, nor used as a source for any form of machine learning including AI datasets, without the prior written permission of the publisher.

The publisher and the author have made every effort to obtain permissions for any third party material used in this book and to comply with copyright law. Any queries in this respect should be brought to the attention of the publisher and any omissions will be corrected in future editions.

A CIP catalogue record for this book is available from the British Library.

Paperback ISBN: 9781036705244

Printed and bound in Great Britain by Clays Ltd, Elcograf S.p.A.

Chapter One

For five days she hadn't killed anyone, hadn't even thought about guns. Five days wasn't the longest she'd ever gone, but in recent months, it counted as a record.

Wen Sung, a former top Chinese spy, had been trained and employed by the Ministry of State Security, China's CIA equivalent. The MSS had first recruited her as a teenager, and for nearly ten years, she'd done their worst.

She looked over at her boyfriend and smiled. It had been a wonderful break, but now they needed to return to the real world.

"We could stay longer," the tech billionaire said, moving a wisp of shiny black hair away from her beautifully chiseled face. Chase Malone, an inventor and engineer, comfortable in worn, but tailored khaki pants and an open shirt, grabbed Wen around her waist and pulled them together on the rock they perched on, gazing out at a scenic lake. At age twenty-nine, he'd seen the end not of his career, but of everything, and so had dropped out of the Silicon Valley fast track. After creating breakthrough technologies in AI, machine learning, and cognitive-predictive computer applications, he saw that the continual misuse of his inventions, and other advanced technologies, would eventually spell the end of humanity. After reuniting with Wen and dodging the MSS, Chase and Wen had made a decision to use their talents and connections to prevent people from using technology to do more harm—or, rather, the decision had been made *for* them after a series of events which included being pursued by an unknown group for reasons not entirely clear.

"We're almost out of food," Wen said, glancing at their backpacks.

"How about we live off the land?"

She gave him a 'get serious' look. The two of them had gone off-grid and vanished more than a year earlier, only surfacing when something required them to intervene.

"Okay, but we could hike out, get some more provisions, then hit the trail, find another lake . . . "

"Let's go find another island," Wen suggested.

"Deal."

In order to mend their wounds, relax, and spend a few days alone, a luxury they had only been allowed a few times, they'd spent four days camping by a sub-Alpine lake in the Marble Mountains wilderness of California. They hadn't seen another soul the entire time. The solitude and crystal waters of the lake had cleansed them.

Before the backpack trip, they had been in San Francisco, helping Chase's business partner, Desmond "Dez" Jefferson, with some of the technical aspects of Balance Engineering, their increasingly secretive company.

"It was great seeing your mom," Wen said. "I'm so glad we got to visit her before we came up here."

"Me too, so we could borrow all their camping gear. I'm

amazed she saved it. She and my dad haven't been backpacking in years." His expression turned sad. People who had been pursuing Chase and Wen had killed his father not long ago, and badly injured his mother.

"Your mom's looking really good. She seems to be doing okay," Wen said, trying to lighten the mood.

"She's worried about me," Chase said. "She didn't say so, but I can see it's stressful for her."

"Boone said he's talked to her about it. It's not like it's exactly our *choice* to live this way," Wen said, mentioning Chase's older brother, Boone.

Feeling a bit sad to be leaving the wilderness, they talked about how great it would be to build a cabin up there, or somewhere similar, where no one could find them. But they both knew it was a dream that would never come true. They had too much to do, there were too many problems to solve, and somebody would find them anyway. Somebody always did.

A couple hours into their hike out, Wen spotted trouble. "There's somebody out there," she said quietly.

"Are you serious?" But Chase knew she was. He just couldn't believe that someone had found them again. No one knew where they were, *no one*.

"Four hundred yards."

"Where?" Chase whispered as they kept hiking as before.

"Up ahead in that clearing. Tree. Left."

Chase scanned the area without moving his head, his eyes concealed behind his sunglasses, but couldn't find anyone.

"He's going to get us," Wen said, her eyes darting, searching for other hostiles. "He'll have an open shot in another minute."

Chapter Two

So far, Wen didn't see any other threats, but they were still walking straight into the sniper's trap.

"I've only got my Glock," Wen said, referring to her favorite pistol, a Glock 19. Normally she liked to carry at least three weapons, two of them being submachine guns, but hadn't anticipated needing them. The only threat they had expected was the possibility of running into a bear.

"I'll drop down to the river and go that way," Chase said, knowing already that Wen would be planning to head up into the woods to find the sniper. Even if they could have both escaped without a confrontation, they needed to know who had sent him and why. "I'll see if anyone else is aiming for us."

"I'll head up," she replied.

"I know."

There was absolutely nothing that bothered Chase more than when they had to be strategically separated. He had never liked it, but by now knew not to debate it with Wen because it was the way she had been trained, and, more importantly, it had saved their lives more times than he cared to remember.

She smiled. "I'll see you on the other side. Let's try to meet at the cattle guard, but if one of us isn't there, second spot is where the trail turns back into the wider gravel road." She blew him a kiss.

He nodded, blew a kiss back, left the trail, and hiked down toward Shackleford Creek, which rapidly descended nearly two thousand feet over five miles, with noisy cascades, drops, waterfalls, and rapids making a frothy mix of white water, moss, evergreens, and crystal pools.

Even with her pack, Wen moved through the trees as if invisible, but planned to abandon it once she got closer to the sniper. Counting steps, checking the breeze, watching how the shadows fell, the angle of the ground's slope, movement of the birds, Wen, now on auto-pilot, took it all in, processing the probabilities and ingredients of the fluid situation that was going to end in a death—hers or his.

The sniper cursed. In thirty more feet, there would have been a clear shot and he could've gone home. He had it all visualized—the woman would fall first, then he'd catch the man on the run. If it all went well, two shots would do it, though the man, moving, might take one more. Either way, they would be dead, he'd photograph the bodies, cut off a finger from each of them, and put them in separate Ziploc bags. Based on the time, he might've been able to get paid that night, but now he wouldn't until the following day. The two targets, for some reason, had suddenly gone off trail. He wondered for a second if they had spotted him, but didn't see how that was possible since he was virtually invisible—a special forces trained sniper hidden in a camouflage blind.

He decided to wait a few minutes to see what was going on. There was a good chance they were both going off to relieve themselves. It made sense why the guy had gone to one side and the woman to the other.

He lost sight of them.

Surely they'll return to the trail shortly. He waited. *Never break the blind, maintain the zone.*

When he heard a twig snap in front of him, he immediately looked behind him, but it was too late.

Wen landed on top of the sniper, his Barrett M95 rifle slid away, and before he could reach his Beretta 92SB-F sidearm, she had it. It had all happened in an instantaneous blur. Her Glock pointed at his neck. He thought about tossing her, he was much larger, but the fierce determination in her eyes and something more—she'd been trained, he realized—stopped him. The better chance at survival was to hold still. She hadn't killed him yet. She wanted something.

Wen, her knees on his chest, watched his pupils dilate, saw the muscles in his neck jump and the slight movement of his mouth as she read the thoughts and plans of her prisoner, and knew she didn't have much time. "Who sent you?"

"I don't know."

"If you truly don't know, then I'm going to kill you." Her eyes narrowed. "So, I'm asking you one more time. *Who* sent you?"

"I *really* don't know. It doesn't work that way. I get the job through an intermediary."

"Who's that?"

"I can't tell you."

"I thought you said he was just an intermediary." She pushed the Glock harder against his throat.

"He is, but if I tell you, I'm as good as dead."

"You're as good as dead right now if you don't. I'm counting to three."

"A guy named Miller. He's in Los Angeles."

"You're lying."

"I am not."

Wen pulled the trigger. "Yes, you are," she said, but the man was already dead. For a moment, Wen thought she heard what sounded like the flapping of thousands of wings . . . but instantly, the forest was more silent than before.

Chapter Three

Wen caught up with Chase for the last half-mile of the trail back to the car.

"I heard the gunshot," Chase said, feeling himself shift, yet again, from intense fear to intense relief.

"Were you worried?"

"Always, but I've learned to recognize the sound of your Glock, so I knew the chances were good that you had been the one to fire."

"Even before you heard the gun, you should've known I would prevail."

"I did," he said, taking her hand. "What happened?"

Wen explained how she questioned the man and that he had lied twice. Chase knew the MSS did extensive psychological training, and that their agents could spot a lie quite easily with a number of tells—such as blinking rapidly in succession, darting eyes, movement of pupils, shaking of the head, and a dozen other indicators.

"Not only was he lying, but he was about to make a move."

"It's too bad," Chase said.

"Yeah," she agreed.

They both lived with the constant threat from people who had been after them for more than a year, and thus far they had been unable to identify or link them to any specific group, company, or government. Along the way there'd been plenty of others pursuing them, but those had belonged to the CIA, the MSS, and companies they'd been involved with at the time. These people—who they called "shadow people"—were something different, and they worried that, sooner or later, their luck, Wen's skills, or Chase's brains, were going to run out.

"The sniper had no ID on him whatsoever," Wen continued.

"So we know nothing."

"I did take both his weapons, and even dug the slug that went through the bastard's neck out of a root."

"Sometimes you scare me," Chase said.

"Sometimes?" She laughed, but then her expression turned sad.

He regretted making the comment. Wen, an efficient trained killer, probably one of the best in the world, didn't enjoy her work. Chase knew how emotionally taxing it was for her to take a life. That trauma was one of the reasons they came to the mountains, hoping for some peace and to escape the violent adventure their life had become. He was angry at the irony that they had been attacked after such a blissful five days, and that she had to kill again. "I'm sorry," he said softly.

Wen knew he wasn't apologizing for the comment, but for another death she'd endured. "Me too."

"He's bound to have a vehicle down here," Chase said, as they were nearing the final gate that kept the free-roaming cattle from invading the parking area for the trailhead.

"And there's a good chance his ID is in it," Wen added.

Just before they opened the gate, while they were still in a stand of lichen covered trees and ponderosa pines, Chase held out an arm to stop her. "You see that silver Jeep Renegade?" he whispered. "There's a guy in it."

"Someone waiting to make sure the hit job got done."

"We'll have to get to the car without being seen," Chase said.

"I think we can get around. He's parked in the front row, we're in the back . . . if we go around these trees we can get to the car before he notices."

"As soon as we start the engine and pull out . . . " Chase began.

"I'll have the gun pointed right at him."

Chase knew it wouldn't be too difficult for Wen to sneak up behind the Jeep and kill the man without even using her gun, and they would be able to have a safer escape. However, if they could avoid another killing, they were going to try.

"If we get enough of a head start . . . "

"And I can shoot out his tires . . . "

While sitting low in the front seat, Chase started the vehicle. Wen, in the passenger seat, leaned out the open door, ready to shoot the tires, still wishing she had her MP7 submachine gun.

The man spotted them right away, but didn't have a gun ready, so Chase steered out of the parking lot before he could respond. Wen fired toward him, but she couldn't get a steady aim while their Subaru Outback bounced over the roots and ruts of the old logging road.

The man slammed the Jeep in reverse, backed over a

small log and into a ditch, and jumped up to the road, fishtailing in a plume of dust. It was impossible for Wen to hit his tires under those conditions.

Chase gripped the wheel tightly as the Subaru blasted down the road that, in most spots, was only six inches wider then its wheelbase. The crumbling, rocky road descended seven miles toward Mugginsville. Chase, who liked to tell people he was a professional race car driver, normally reveled in a good race, but this road was about as treacherous as he could imagine—unless it started to snow, or maybe if the nearby Mount Shasta erupted. The loose surface fell away eight hundred feet down through crags and trees to a sure death. He pushed the car as fast as he could, trying to gain a bigger lead.

The Jeep's only real advantage was clearance, he thought as the Subaru bottomed out on a dip, then bounced along a rare straight stretch of dusty washboard.

"I should've shot him in the parking lot," Wen said. "We've got six miles of this still ahead," she said, looking back at the Renegade, now only two hundred feet behind, "and when we get down to the main road, it'll be nearly impossible to lose him."

"I'm sure not going to worry about that now" Chase said, checking the rearview mirror. The Jeep was barreling toward them. "I think he means to ram us."

"If he hits us at the wrong moment, we'll go careening over the edge." Wen leaned out and fired, pressing her advantage. She could concentrate on shooting while the driver of the Jeep had to concentrate on driving. *On these roads, it's nearly impossible to shoot and drive at the same time.* Yet as soon as that thought came, somehow the man managed to get a shot off. It didn't come close to hitting the Subaru, but that wasn't his intention. It was a warning that he could both shoot and drive.

A minute later, the shooting didn't matter, as he smashed the Jeep's flat steel bumper into the Subaru. The jolt sent them several feet off course, and one of the front tires hung halfway over the edge before Chase righted it and got back on the road, instantly swerving to avoid a fallen boulder. He hit the gas to escape another ramming, and ran across several chunky rocks—one of them tearing through the wheel-well. Chase over-corrected.

"We're going over the cliff!" Wen screamed.

Chapter Four

The Subaru headed perilously toward the ledge without enough road remaining to make the turn. Chase caught the steering wheel and cranked it back hard, and through a crazy bit of time-stopping magic that he could never explain, the Subaru, with two wheels going over, somehow found enough traction to get around and back on the road.

"How did you do that?" Wen yelled.

"I have no idea!"

"He's coming back!"

"If he gets us on the right turn, next time we're really going over."

"Drive faster," Wen said as he rammed them again.

"Going fast is the same thing as him pushing us off the edge! There's just not enough road."

Wen fired another shot, aiming for the tires, but as the Subaru jostled over the rocks and ruts, the bullet hit the passenger side of the Jeep's windshield. "That'll slow him down a little," she said. "But he's got bulletproof glass!"

Still, the windshield was now hard to see through, and the Jeep immediately slowed.

Chase shouted two words of profanity. Wen turned as Chase slammed on the brakes. A giant horse trailer being towed by an oversized pickup crawled ahead of them.

Chase pounded the horn. "That thing's way too big to navigate this ridiculous excuse for a road!"

"The man in the Jeep will be able to *walk* faster than us." Wen took aim, but the Jeep came up hard and rammed them. Chase alternated between gas and brake pedals, but slid on the loose scree and tapped the back of the horse trailer. It was impossible to know if the trailer-driver even noticed.

"Somewhere the road has to open up," Wen said. "I remember on our way in there were some pull-outs."

"This isn't a road, it's a damned bike path," Chase muttered.

The Jeep was going slow enough that its driver could easily fire at them. Two bullets hit the side and back of the car.

"He's shooting," Wen shouted, "but not very well!"

"Let's hope he doesn't get better with practice," Chase said, checking the speedometer, which was dancing between four and six mph.

Suddenly a pull off opened on the cliff side of the road. The horse trailer should've gone in, but didn't. At the last instant, Chase took it, whipping around the side of the trailer. Wen looked out her window, straight down, as rocks dropped off over the ledge, cascading into the trees hundreds of feet below. The Jeep foolishly tried to follow. The back right passenger side wheel went off the road, hanging in the air, before Chase gunned it and brought the Subaru flying around in front of the horse trailer. The pickup truck driver hit his breaks at the same moment, causing the Jeep to miss the opening.

Two wheels went over, as if in slow motion. The driver hit the accelerator, spraying gravel, rock, dirt, and dust, as he fought to get traction back on the road. He didn't, and the Jeep rolled off the side.

Wen looked back in time to see the Jeep's driver trying to climb out of his door before the vehicle rolled the rest of the way, crushing his body as it crashed into the canyon, landing in a twisted wreck, crumpled around a giant tree.

"Instant karma," Chase said. "Never pays to be a tailgater."

"His own doing," Wen said, glad she hadn't killed him.

Once back in civilization, Wen inserted new SIM cards into their disposable burner phones, then called to check messages. Chase drove them north into Oregon, where he had a private plane and pilots waiting at the Medford International Airport. He'd long ago given up buying planes that were too easily traced, and instead leased them through a complex series of shell companies and identities managed by a small team of key employees.

Wen put the phone on speaker to take a call from Margot, the leader of WOLF—sometimes simply referred to as "The Cause"—a group of people seeking to bring about more income equality throughout the world. Whenever Margot called, it usually meant trouble of some kind. However, as soon as Margot said she had a message from Mei Lein, a woman who'd helped her escape China, Wen knew this time it was far worse than simply trouble. Her worst nightmare had actually come true.

Chapter Five

Wen instinctively checked the side view mirror as Chase drove north on I-5. *Just because two assassins are laying dead in the Marble Mountains, doesn't mean we're safe. There will be more. There are always more.*

"Who is Mei Lein?" Chase asked.

"She's with WOLF, in China. She's actually the one who recruited me into The Cause, and . . . she helped me escape."

"Then why is it so horrible that she wants you to call her?"

"Because Mei Lein would never risk contacting me unless something awful had happened and she needed help. I don't exist anymore, remember?"

"What kind of help?"

"She must be in trouble, if she's risking contact with me now." Wen pulled out another phone, switched its SIM card, and punched in three separate multi-digit codes to make the phone untraceable. They had a system which routed calls through servers in Argentina, South Africa, and

Greenland via a special satellite, and then to Hong Kong, where finally it would connect to the number in China.

"Thank you for calling," Mei Lein said in Mandarin, her voice filled with relief.

"Of course. What's wrong?" Wen asked in Mandarin. The brief conversation held in their native tongue quickly turned to the urgent matter that had prompted the risky communication.

"Mǐng Rénshēng is a secret program involving many scientists. The Chinese government is far more advanced in human gene editing than anyone can believe."

"Can you switch to English?" Wen asked. "So that Chase can hear?"

Mei Lein repeated her statement, and then also translated Mǐng Rénshēng, meaning, "To Command Life."

Wen brought up the infamous case of Chinese scientist He Jiankui, who, in late November 2018, announced that he had successfully completed human embryo gene editing, altering the DNA of twin girls before birth. Academics, medical professionals, and scientists worldwide had condemned the experimental procedure.

"No, no, that was nothing. The Chinese government lies. He was not the first one, that was just a test case to gauge opinion . . . Jiankui is doing nothing new. They are much further along than he claims. Hundreds of scientists are working on Mǐng Rénshēng."

"So you're saying they've done more than just those twins?" Chase asked.

"Many, many more. And not just embryos, but adults, too."

"Adults?" Chase echoed, shocked. Embryos were one thing, but editing genes in adults was thought to be decades away.

"It is very dangerous," Mei Lein continued. "They are not just trying to cure disease . . . the communist Chinese government is intent on creating a master race."

Wen and Chase looked at each other with deep concern.

"A master race of super Chinese?" Wen asked.

Hearing it from Wen, it sunk in, and Chase looked at her as if she'd just announced Hitler had escaped the bunker in 1945.

"Yes," Mei Lein answered. "And it's worse than you can imagine."

Wen couldn't imagine *how* it could be worse—the fastest growing economy and military in the world, a country essentially run by a dictator, and one that could soon be the most powerful on earth, had the capability, and was now pursuing the development of a genetically altered master race. It sounded like a horror movie.

"Can you come to China?" Mei Lein asked, in a tone that fully expressed she understood what the request meant.

Wen and Chase shared another glance, one that conveyed terror.

"You know how risky that would be for me!" Wen said quietly. Mount Shasta's ephemeral stance offered a strange power, one that neither comforted nor clarified the danger they faced. "Can't someone there help?" Wen felt horrible by not just saying yes immediately to a friend whom she owed so much, knowing she never would've called if there were another way. But the risks of returning to China were enormous. She had to ask.

"I am sorry to put you in this position, Wen, but they have cracked down, and arrested so many. Those of us still working are under constant surveillance and monitoring, but you could come invisibly. You do not exist. We would give you what support we can. I very much understand if you cannot do this."

"Of course we will try to find a way." Wen looked at Chase. He nodded slightly, though was incredibly apprehensive about the idea. There could be no riskier place in the world for them than mainland China, and to do so in order to undermine one of the communist government's greatest and most secret objectives made it even more of a suicide mission.

Chapter Six

The Minister of State Security Peoples Republic of China, Li Dazhao, inspected the BioCheng facility with five MSS lieutenants. BioCheng, one of China's premier scientific installations, was the lead laboratory and research center for the Mìng Rénshēng program. It, and all other facilities in the program, fell under the MSS security apparatus. A sweeping campus, located between Beijing and Tianjin, the buildings connected through a series of underground tunnels. More than any other, BioCheng was a vital piece of China's ambitions to control the future.

Li, whose job it was to protect China's interests, smiled, because unlike the artificial islands his country was building in the South China Sea, missile installations, nuclear weapons systems, and the long list of record-breaking engineering projects such as giant dams, major electrical plants, towering skyscrapers, and huge industrial centers, the interiors of these buildings were free from surveillance by their enemies. No matter how many satellites the Americans put into space, they would not be able to see what was going on inside these labs, inside these microscopes, and neither the CIA nor the NSA could get into the lab's computers because they were not linked to any network.

Dr. Tián, the head scientist, had shown him during many briefings on the Mìng Rénshēng program, that gene editing was the most powerful and promising way China would dominate the coming century and beyond.

Shen Hán, Minister Li's top lieutenant, asked about the Americans lagging behind in artificial intelligence, bio engineering research, and quantum computing.

"All along," Li began, "the problem with the Americans has been that they are merely concerned about today and tomorrow. Their great planners only look ahead five years. Although sometimes they might talk of twenty years into the future, Americans never maintain their goals and objectives for that long."

"Three to five years is usually their limit," Shen agreed.

"Whereas, of course, in China, we think of decades as being the present, and in terms of centuries as being the future. Our long view has always looked into the millennia."

"That, as well as China's massive population, is our advantage, yet the rest of the world never sees this."

Dr. Tián, the chief scientist at BioCheng, began the presentation. "This lab, along with sixty-three others, maintains the highest security standards of information and data share. Our system is automated, encrypted, courier-based."

Minister Li had been nervous about the need for the labs to exchange data on a regular basis, and had created the courier system, where highly vetted individuals were given encrypted drives that were hand-delivered whenever needed. Most were done via bullet train transfers, although helicopters and cars were also used. They were considering launching a drone program, thereby eliminating the human element, something Li had been pushing.

Li nodded his approval, although, as usual, he was already contemplating weaknesses in their internal security. He didn't need to point out any of the flaws today, but made mental notes. Li rarely needed to write anything down. His memory, logic, and ability for deduction were that superior. Li also lived and died by the digital and paper trails of others, and was loath to leave one himself unless absolutely necessary.

Shen Hán was actually Li's closest lieutenant, one of the few he truly trusted—at least as much as he could trust anyone in his position. Shen was attending the walk-through with different concerns than the minister. Several times, Shen had voiced doubts about the leadership and scientists ignoring the tremendous ethical, and potentially disastrous, ramifications of Mìng Rénshēng.

On the way to the presentation, Shen had asked Li again, "What will happen when mistakes are made?" Shen had a background in science and knew that nobody understood the far-reaching consequences of altering genes. "They are interfering with evolution."

"Our job is to protect the secrets and guard their progress." Li's resolute stare ahead didn't hide the fragment of a concern in the bare squint his baggy eyes made—really the only hint of stress or ill health on his otherwise thin and fit body.

"You and I see different dangers, Minister," he said in hushed tones, as the two of them trailed behind the tour in a long underground corridor.

At the same time Li listened to Shen, he silently listed the things that he would like to change—the corridors had air vents, too many doors, there should be guards . . .

"Ours is not to question the science," Li cautioned again, yet he had to silently admit that Shen had opened his eyes to some of the dangers, and with his deep love of country, he worried that China could be making a mistake. Still, bringing up the topic at his next meeting with the president brought many risks. In China, questioning established policy and government priorities was often seen as disloyal. Li also worried that the scientists had already gone too far down the road to turn back, and there was the consideration of the other countries who were also secretly pursuing this course.

"What if there is no humanity left for China to lead?" Shen whispered, a distinguished man himself in everything but his high top black basketball sneakers and propensity for cheap candy.

"You must believe we will get this right," Li said quietly, taking a split moment to reiterate his point with a look into his colleague's eye as they reached the end of the corridor. Dr. Tián pressed his palm into the biometric panel and gained access.

"It is too easy for it to go wrong," Shen said, trying to keep his voice low as they walked through the doorway. "The odds of success are one in a million. The odds of failure are nine hundred and ninety-nine thousand in a million."

"But our competitors. You understand how easy it is for anybody to undertake this technology. We must stay ahead."

"It would be better standing with the international community, condemning and monitoring these plans."

"No more on the subject," Li said firmly. "Not now, not here."

Shen, of course, knew better than to press the minister, but they both knew he would broach the subject again.

Although this was not the purview of the MSS, Shen clung to the fact that Li was one of the most powerful men in China—certainly in the top ten, maybe top five. If there was still a chance to stop the program, Li could have influence, and there were opportunities to have influence in covert ways that the minister's rivals would not understand, nor would they be able to discover the origins of the descent. Risky times.

Chapter Seven

On the flight to Hong Kong, Chase recalled another flight he had taken there in his desperate search for Wen, at the time she had just recently fled China. So much had happened since. On the previous flight, he had wondered if they would finally be together after so many years of thinking he'd never see her again. It had been a crazy journey no sane person would have undertaken, yet it worked out, had changed his life for the better . . .

Those thoughts comforted him as he looked ahead at what they might encounter in China now and how much crazier this trip was than the other one had been. Chase worried that this time he was tempting fate too much, and might lose Wen forever.

They'd met as students on his third day at Tsinghua University in Beijing. He'd known a lot of smart women at Stanford, but in addition to Wen's obvious brain power, she possessed a confidence that made her magnetic. Her quiet concentration juxtaposed a firecracker humor and infectious laugh. He fell in love immediately, and again every day thereafter. They studied together and monopolized each other's time. He proposed six months in, and if not for the problem of her being unable to move to the US and him not wanting to live forever in China, they would have wed, he felt sure. He almost took an offer with a Chinese company to stay with her, but it would have just delayed the inevitable and increased his pain. They'd never gotten over each other, and had lost contact for five years, but when she got in terrible trouble and needed him, he'd immediately stopped his extremely successful, complex life and rushed to her.

Suddenly, the familiar voice of the Astronaut on speakerphone brought him back. The Astronaut, whose real name was Nash Graham—a math savant, widely sought out by the world intelligence agencies, including the CIA, NSA, MSS, Russian SVR, and others—possessed a computer-like intelligence, and, like them, lived as a fugitive. Of late, the Astronaut had become part of The Cause, and, more importantly, worked regularly with Chase and Wen—not to mention he was in love with Wen, but he couldn't really love anyone, at least not in an affectionate way. Closeness, love, and tenderness, debilitated him, so his care for Wen had been the closest to a relationship he'd ever known, or likely ever would. He actually felt empathy for her, not a usual mode for him.

Wen had been trying to reach him.

"I think it would be a good idea for me to talk you out of this trip," the Astronaut said. "People like to say America is the most powerful country the world has ever known, but this is only because they have the most sophisticated military in the world, and this fact is not lost on the Chinese, who have been steadily catching up. And yet they already possess the advantage . . . "

"We *have* to go Nash," Chase said.

"That is because you don't know the advantage. Wen doesn't even fully understand it because she was brought up under their control."

"I guess you're going to explain this advantage to us?" Wen said.

"Since you asked."

Wen looked at Chase and smiled, always amused by the Astronaut's ways.

"Unlike the United States," the Astronaut began, "where the power is spread out across three coequal branches of government, including one hundred senators, four hundred and thirty-five representatives, nine Supreme Court Justices, the president, and all the executive branch cabinet members, fifty state governors, state legislatures, and—"

Chase rolled his eyes. "The point?"

"China only has a handful of people, and ultimately only one, that decides everything. Which is why they build buildings faster, grow their military faster, and have come to dominate the world. Wealth is concentrated in the government. They own many of the major enterprises, they run the whole county like a private corporation."

"We know this."

"Listen," the Astronaut said, as if talking to a misbehaving child. "They can spend far more money, and, as they've taken the manufacturing base from America and captured the all-powerful American consumers with their cheap prices, they have been siphoning the world's wealth for decades. *That* is their ultimate advantage. In a sense, you are up against a madman bent on world domination, and unlike the movies where the heroes—you two—prevail after a hopeless and dramatic fight, in the real world, it rarely ends well."

"We can—" Wen began.

"You got away once, my dear Wen. You are asking for quite a lot to think that you can escape a second time."

"But you saw what we sent you," Wen said.

The Astronaut sighed, knowing his words had meant nothing. "Yes, of course. I have done extensive research on the issue, and there is no doubt this is the most immediate threat to humanity. Of course, there is a long list—nuclear weapons, nuclear proliferation, pandemic plagues, artificial intelligence, asteroid strikes, biological weapons . . . "

Chase rolled his eyes again. "But back to the point."

"The point, is you *shouldn't* go to China. But since you two refuse to listen, I am saying that this is a worthy cause to die for, since you surely will."

"Thanks for the vote of confidence," Chase said.

"I'd like to refuse to help you, so I won't feel guilty once you're dead. However, since I know that my assistance will give you a better chance of surviving—and by better chance I mean two-point-thirty-eight percent instead of one-point-twenty-nine percent—I'll do what I can . . . but I will not be attending your funerals."

Chapter Eight

At BioCheng, Minister Li and Shen followed Dr. Tián and the others up a flight of stairs. Li knew, from studying blueprints of the facility, that there were elevators on either end of the building. However, they were rarely used for anything other than freight. He noted that there were not enough cameras. *There are never enough cameras anywhere*, he thought.

Mìng Rénshēng, more than eight years old, had experienced major breakthroughs on a regular basis throughout that time. However, recent developments had prompted renewed attention from MSS. With such a large program, leaks were inevitable, and with them there had been attempts at sabotage. Lately, advances, including successful edits on living human adult genes, had taken the science to a whole new level. Further complicating things was the ill-advised decision to announce the He Jiankui twin embryo procedure. Now, serious international scrutiny had been steadily increasing.

Li tapped the shoulder of one of his other aides and pointed to several areas. The aide understood immediately that the minister wanted cameras installed at those points, and quickly took photos and jotted down the exact locations. Normally, photos were not allowed to be taken in the facility, but, of course, rules didn't apply to the minister.

Once the group had progressed through several more secured doors, they eventually ended up inside the main lab. More than forty scientists in white suits worked with an even larger number of assistants. Dr. Tián referred to "the vault," a glass room with a giant, unconnected computer.

"We load data to and from the couriers in there," Dr. Tián said. "At the other end of the lab is what we call 'The View.'" He pointed to an enclosed space with large monitors.

Only Minister Li, Shen, Dr. Tián, and his deputy entered the vault.

"I know these security protocols very well," Li said. "I designed them myself."

Dr. Tián was aware of this, but his deputy seemed quite impressed, as he temporarily disabled the system.

"Then you'll know that this room is impossible to visit without full authorization," the deputy said, demonstrating, as if he'd rehearsed and been waiting for this moment for weeks. The deputy was not going to let the fact that the minister already knew everything he was going to say deter him from saying it anyway. "You must be one of the authorized scientists, of whom there are twelve. To access this room, the biometric sensor must confirm identity and verify authorization, and then once in the room, it is controlled by pressure sensitive floors and temperature control, so that only one person can be in here at a time."

"There are sonic sensors and cameras monitoring the room twenty-four hours a day," Li added, pleased the deputy was so excited by the room's defenses.

"And the sequential codes are changed on a nonregular basis, two to three times a day, with an alpha-numeric passcode of seventy-two characters, which must be synced to the situation by hand."

"Yes, have there been any issues?" the minister asked.

"Of course not," the deputy said, astonished that there could even potentially be a problem with this kind of security.

As they readied to leave the vault, Li took one final glance at the server machine, the angles of the glass and the cameras, and seemed happy. Still, he made another mental note to double check the specs on the glass once he was back at his office.

As they walked across the lab to The View, Li wondered which one of the forty-three scientists or sixty-eight assistants was the leak. He'd had every single one of their profiles analyzed with every human and AI tool available, yet the rat had not been revealed. He eyed each person with hidden contempt, as if he or she were the villain.

Inside The View, several workstations filled the center area with screens on the walls. Although most of the room was visible through thick bullet-proof glass, the monitors were not. Li had made that mandatory, to avoid assistants without full security clearances from seeing sensitive data.

Dr. Tián gave presentations inside The View. "We have successfully identified the mutant genotypes responsible for these inherited genetic disorders." He pointed to a list. "We then can easily remove or alter the mutant genes in the embryo, so once those subjects are born, they will not be vulnerable to the diseases." Tián cycled through a series of case studies and photos of infants appearing healthy and happy.

"Have there been any ill effects?" Shen asked.

"Not with these cases," Tián said.

"In *any* cases?" Shen pressed.

Dr. Tián looked to the minister, as if unsure whether or not to answer truthfully. Li gave an attentive and expectant look, then nodded slightly.

Tián licked his dry lips. "Not in any of the cases I am involved with. Now, let me show you the next phase. This is very exciting."

"How about any cases that you are aware of?" Shen asked, locking eyes with Tián and holding his stare.

Tián hesitated. "In research, it's all trial and error."

Shen continued to stare without comment.

"Of course, there have been some errors," Tián admitted. "This is how we have progressed to this point. Our success is without question." His voice filled with indignant anger at the audacity of a non-scientist questioning him. "Perhaps you do not understand . . . we are rewriting the rules of *life*."

Chapter Nine

As their plane flew closer to China, Wen could feel the mixed emotions of fear and the internal joy of returning home. It was fear that was winning the inner battle.

"Thank you," Wen said to the Astronaut, for agreeing to help them.

"I've sent you a comprehensive review on CRISPR," he said. "CRISPR is clustered regularly interspaced short palindromic repeats—much easier to say CRISPR, don't you think?"

"Yes." Her tone, even in one word, let the Astronaut know the depth of her trepidations, as he knew her seemingly unlimited strengths.

"CRISPR is what allows scientists to edit DNA by using a cheap and relatively simple technique. It's based on the DNA fragments from viruses that bacteria have learned to defeat. My report details all this and attempts to put it in layman's terms."

"What about the Chinese program?"

"I put in a section on what we know about Ming

Rénshēng and other attempts around the world. I should caution you that we don't have much data on the Chinese program because, as I said, they have that advantage, and they only release what they want us to know. The communist government has thousands more spies than we do. It's an uphill battle."

"But we have you," Wen said sweetly into the phone. She knew the Astronaut had a certain affection for her, and that if she and Chase died, he would be one of the people who missed her the most.

"I have managed to get into Ghost Dragon," the Astronaut continued, referring to a 2100-class communications satellite and the secretive spy network routed through it. Ghost Dragon's software had originally been developed by the US National Security Agency for the CIA "Heaven" network; however, the Chinese stole it and developed the advanced system further, making it considerably more sophisticated. "But I've only been able to hold it for certain intervals, obviously trying not to attract their attention . . . to me, or what we're after."

"How far did you get?" Chase asked.

"I have ascertained certain positions of MSS activity and high security, plus their database, which I will send over to Mars."

Chase's oldest friend, Mars, a forty-three-year-old convict at Lompoc Federal Prison, had four years remaining on a "dime" sentence. He'd developed a method to help keep Chase's whereabouts unknown by utilizing a system called "decoying." Reports and sightings of Chase would occur at random intervals across the globe. The many people looking for him would get a constant stream of bad information. Through credit card use, surveillance cameras linked to facial recognition data bases, and a number of other related methods, the sightings would flood in at critical times and overwhelm those seeking Chase.

"I assume you'll be using vIDs," the Astronaut said, with a certain amount of pride in his voice. The virtual Image Deviation system was an incredible collaborative invention, jointly created by the Astronaut and Chase. Its purpose was to fool the algorithms that powered facial recognition cameras. The ingenious spray-on application covered a subject's face with hundreds of nano micro-processors, each thinner than a human hair. The translucent gold specks were virtually undetectable to the naked eye.

"Of course, it's our only way in. But, as you know, we've never tested it in China."

"This will be a good test then. However, if it fails, this will be the last test."

They told the Astronaut their plans, so he could begin working initial routes and looking for weak points in the surveillance state. "What are you going to do for weapons?"

Chase and Wen had a network of people who provided them weapons and other materials in most countries they visited. They affectionately referred to them as a delivery of "groceries," but their suppliers did not operate in China.

"WOLF will be helping with that," Wen replied, looking out the plane's window as familiar buildings locked in her eyesight and clenched her stomach.

"I've already spent some time trying to search databases, and I've sent you my results. In a directory of all known scientists in the field, the leading candidates have spoken publicly at symposiums, forums, conferences, and are likely not the people you're looking for."

"Hopefully our local contacts can assist with identifying the targets," Wen said, entwining her fingers with Chase's.

"What is your objective, by the way? Surely you're not planning to assassinate a hundred scientists?"

"No, there would only be more scientists," Chase replied. "We have to stop the source."

"The source?"

"The Chinese government." His voice hushed suddenly.

"Same issue. Kill the president, they bring in another."

"No, the only way we have is to find the program they've hidden in the darkness, and bring it into the light," Chase said. "If we show it to the world, and they see its dangers, perhaps the world can force China to stop."

"How?" the Astronaut asked.

"I'm thinking boycotts, embargoes—totally isolate China unless they agree to full disclosure and inspections. And there'll have to be an international treaty on the use of gene editing. If it's not fully transparent around the globe, then some rogue nation, greedy corporation, or extreme terrorist will make a mistake and end us all."

"That's an ambitious mission, if undertaken," the Astronaut said. "You're going to need a lot of help from the US government, and many others, in order to make that work. Nothing simple about it, with all those diverse interests."

"Exactly," Wen said. "That is why we have to get the proof of what they're doing, and enough data and evidence to shock the world. If we do, then the rest will have to follow, because various priorities and selfishness must fall away when everybody sees and understands the consequences to humanity for letting this get out of control."

"You saw the uproar when news of the He Jiankui twins broke," Chase said. "This is exponentially worse. If we can find what we're looking for, it'll shock and terrify every human on earth."

"That's your best chance," the Astronaut said. "One of the greatest motivators is fear. Good luck Snowdens."

Chapter Ten

Shen looked around at the monitors, inside The View, showing images of gene altered babies, and allowed a forced smile.

"I am quite aware of what you are doing with Mìng Rénshēng," Shen said. "That is precisely why my questions are not to be ignored."

The warning from a top MSS official was not lost on Dr. Tián.

"Of course. Have I satisfied your curiosity, then?"

"Hardly. The errors you mentioned, they have occurred on human embryos, correct?"

Once again, Dr. Tián looked to Minister Li, hoping for a reprieve. Li gave no indication that Tián would be excused from the questioning.

"We have seen many errors on different animals through the years as the program progressed, and in coordination with human errors—I mean trials."

Shen, bringing with him the full intimidation implied by his MSS position, glared at the scientist. "I would like you to *directly* answer my question. How many errors have there been on human subjects?"

He hesitated. "That would be hard to say."

Li stepped closer to Dr. Tián. "Estimate for us, please." But the word please had none of the normal graciousness associated with a friendly request. Rather, it suddenly sounded like a threat.

"Perhaps a thousand, more or less," Dr. Tián said, with a clear look of shame."

"What happened to them?" Shen asked.

Dr. Tián shook his head.

"They are all dead?"

"Yes." Dr. Tián looked toward the door, then the ground, and finally to the monitor still filled with babies.

"Where are the records of those experiments?" Shen asked.

"The subjects are dead," Li said, shaking his head to Shen.

"It is of no matter," Dr. Tián said. "The records are of no matter."

"I would like to see them," Shen said.

Dr. Tián appeared confused.

"This is not an area for our concern," Minister Li said firmly.

Shen started to say something, about to argue that they could not do complete security if they didn't understand the program and its weaknesses, but Minister Li held up a hand, as if to echo his earlier words: 'Not now, not here.'

Shen took a deep breath, clenched his fists. He knew how things worked. Those records, if they still existed, would be destroyed by the end of the day. As soon as Dr. Tián reported to his superiors that an MSS officer had been asking for them, they would disappear. It was the way in

China, and, he suspected, in most corrupt bureaucracies in the world. Still, deciding whether or not he could push his boss any further, he looked at the scientist, clearly assessing his character, searching for another flaw or weakness, but before he could speak, the minister acted.

"Please, continue the presentation." This time the word 'please' sounded more typical. However, it was laced with an implicit command to move on, meant for both Dr. Tián and Shen.

Dr. Tián happily obliged, showing more successes, and briefly skirting the even more controversial aspects of Míng Rénshēng when he showed that in the future they would be able to select traits for babies, enhance athletic ability, and perhaps remove criminal, rebellious, and other nonconformist traits from people which would, in turn, make a more harmonious society, one free from crime.

Fifteen minutes later, they were in another corridor, which would eventually lead to the exit. Once they were alone in the parking lot, waiting for Minister Li's driver to pull around, Shen could no longer hold his tongue. His muscular frame and uncharacteristic tallness fell short of his pending concern. He could not hold back the emotion he felt for the gravity of the situation.

"You see what they are doing, the dangers they are playing with. Manipulations of biology rarely turn out well—and by rarely I mean *never*." He paced in a short area around Li, trying to relax himself by consistently dropping his shoulders.

"You pushed too far back there," the minister said, speaking barely loud enough to be heard. Li's stress was amazingly controlled, and only compensated in the high sodium diet his doctor told him to be cautious of.

"I had to."

"No."

"They have gone too far."

"This is not our place."

"It's out of control. One thousand errors—*human* errors—it's probably more like *ten* thousand. There must be reconsideration before it is too late."

"The president, and the committee, have decided. Are you suggesting you know more than the president, than the committee?" the minister asked his favorite lieutenant, clearly irritated.

"I am only suggesting that the president and the committee do not fully understand the science, and that their long-view is not as long as it needs to be. And that—"

"Enough."

"They are playing God."

"And you, Shen Hán, what are you playing?"

"I speak for humanity."

"Who appointed you to that position? Why do you think you know more than the other scientists who have far more advanced degrees and experience than you?"

"Because I—"

"Why is it that you second-guess China? Our scientists might just get this right. We may actually *improve* the future of humanity."

"Because it is going too *fast*. No one, not even Dr. Tián, or the President, understand the ramifications, the complications . . ."

"Then why are they pursuing this?"

"They are driven by fear that someone will get ahead, that this is too important to be second-place. And that fear is blinding them to the dangers."

"No more. You say no more on the subject, until I ask you."

"But—" Shen knew he'd overstepped. They stood still, facing each other, the sun high in a cloudless sky, beads of sweat on Shen's linear cheek bones. On Li, there was not a droplet to be seen.

The minister fired a hundred bullets into him with his eyes, and it was enough. Shen bowed his head and went silent, but Li continued to stare until Shen said, "Yes, sir."

Chapter Eleven

The next call Chase received on the plane was from Mars. Mars, a lifelong friend, was an expert at beating artificial intelligence facial recognition systems, CIA tracking, NSA surveillance of devices, and the like. Mars helped Chase and Wen remain invisible, especially when they travelled. Long prior to his conviction, Mars had worked for Chase's mother's auto repair business, and been like an older brother to Chase.

Being behind bars normally meant all communications were monitored and there was zero access to cell phones. However, Mars had carved out a business in prison, with several guards on his "payroll." Mars couldn't always get a phone, but he'd arranged many advantages that could be bought in any corrupt prison system, including the world's largest—the American system, which held more than 2.3 million people, giving it the highest incarceration rate of any country.

Chase had sent Mars a message through a compromised prison official, who got word to the case officer in charge of

Mars. The note contained only four words: *Need help inside China.*

"This doesn't mean you're *going* to China?" Mars asked, cracking his gum loudly.

"Yeah."

Chase heard him spit, probably the piece of gum he was chewing. "Are you crazy?"

"Look, I just argued with the Astronaut," Chase said. Mars and the Astronaut had become acquainted over the last six months while both worked to help Chase and Wen stay off the radar. Mars liked to joke that, "*One day, the Astronaut will visit Mars . . . get it?*"

"So you're just going to have to assume that I know what I'm doing," Chase said, defending his decision.

"You know what they say about people who assume?" Mars said. "And I've known you since you were a kid, so I know that you don't often have any idea what you're doing, and you do it anyway . . . Of course, that's probably the number one reason you became a billionaire, but a lot of dead people, who died in tragic ways, share that trait."

"You're rambling."

"It's just that you have a billion dollars, Chase. Can't you hire a hundred people to go do whatever the hell it is you have to do in China?"

"You know the answer to that."

Mars did know. Chase had always believed if you wanted something done right, do it yourself, and in spite of his half-joking commentary about Chase in their childhood, he had enormous respect for Wen and Chase. They seemed to have a perfect skill set for what they did, and left a small enough footprint to be able to accomplish what others could not. Mars had spent enough time keeping Chase and Wen invisible—and therefore alive—that he'd learned not to underestimate them. Nevertheless, in prison he was surrounded by people who had taken one too many chances and then gotten caught.

Suddenly a softness to his usual gruff and sarcastic banter gave weight to his undeniable love for this close friend. "Please don't go."

"We're already on our way . . . too late to turn back now."

Mars also knew that argument was pointless. "I really have no contacts to speak of in China. I'm not sure how much help I can be. Hopefully vIDs will keep you from being identified—unless China's got something in their program you didn't anticipate."

That thought was one of Chase's greatest worries about the trip. Once again, he was relying on something he'd invented to protect them, and yet, that same technology could be misused in the way the Chinese had set up a surveillance state that had been described by experts as something light years ahead of what any master dystopian storyteller could have created, making Big Brother, from Orwell's *1984,* look like something out of a nursery rhyme.

"I think it'll be important to step up sightings of us in other parts of the world, because the Chinese system is linked to different networks and the AI crossmatches," Chase said, knowing vIDs had a number of vulnerabilities. The Chinese system could easily be more sophisticated than anything they'd tested vIDs against, there could also be problems reapplying the vIDs spray "mask," it could even come off if they should wind up in a river or lake, and finally, a glitch or shut down in any of the vIDs nano processors would make the "masks" worthless. "If vIDs fails and they get close to recognizing us, their system will be working toward a confirmed identity, and at the same time they'll search world databases for a disqualifying match, right? So if I'm spotted in Rome, the algorithm will put less weight on me being the target of the facial recognition and positive ID matching."

"That's easy. What else?"

"I was hoping you could access some of the Chinese dissidents and prisoners there—"

"Wait a minute . . . I know you people on the outside think that all us prisoners are one big family, all connected —and, to a point, in the US, it's true. We have ways of communicating with each other through the "prison telegraph." China, on the other hand, is a whole different world. That said, there are Chinese nationals in our prisons that can communicate with home, and maybe some dissidents there. Still, I think it would be way too slow to help you."

"All right, but can you work on it?"

"I've got nothing but time, you know."

"I know." Chase felt horrible that someone he considered a brother was locked away in prison, and used to avoid asking him for help, but Mars had made it clear, many times, that the more he could do for Chase, the less he felt like a prisoner.

"How's your mom?" Mars asked.

"Physically, she's recovered. I was just there a few days ago. Mentally, she's still pretty wrecked. And misses Dad horribly."

"You do, too."

"Yeah," Chase said, not wanting to allow himself to dwell on the loss of his father too long, especially when he was about to walk into the valley of death, and hoped to come out on the other side.

"And Boone?" Mars asked. The two of them had been

very close years ago. "He came down here not long after Dad was killed, to talk to me about it in person, but I haven't seen him since."

"He spends a lot of time with Mom. His business is going great. He hardly has to be there anymore."

"Yeah, who'd ever thought you could make millions cleaning windows?" Mars said, laughing. Boone's company had secured contracts for cleaning the exterior windows of most of the skyscrapers in San Francisco, and recently in several other western cities. "Next time you talk to him, do me a favor and ask him to bring your mom down to visit me, and tell him to ask her to bring that cinnamon apple fudge, mmm! Nothing like it."

"I'll do that," Chase replied. "I think that would do her a lot of good."

"Meanwhile, don't give her another funeral to go to. Know what I mean?"

"Yeah," Chase said. "I'll live through this if it's the last thing I ever do."

Chapter Twelve

Chase and Wen's plane landed in Hong Kong, where, under false identities, and both wearing vIDs "digital masks," they boarded a commercial flight to Shanghai.

"If we get caught, they'll execute me," was the last thing Wen whispered to Chase before they landed in Hong Kong, and her words echoed in his head as they went through three checkpoints and passed more than sixty cameras—each scrutinizing the structure of their faces, distance between their eyes, and hundreds of other data points to identify and track them.

Only when the flight to Shanghai reached cruising altitude did they relax a little. "So far, so good," Chase said quietly, thinking how far there was still to go.

The vIDs spray—a clear, pump-mist application, consisting of hundreds of nano processors which worked together with an app on their phones—had been designed to completely thwart the facial recognition programs by overtaking the algorithms and providing a "non-match." It had not been field tested in China.

"Hope this works," Wen said.

"The vIDs system has been successfully used in fifty-four major airports," Chase said.

"Not China," Wen reminded him.

"We just got through Hong Kong."

"Hong Kong is the eighth busiest airport in the world," Wen continued, as if describing a small garage. "The largest terminal anywhere on the globe is at Beijing Daxing International, the world's second busiest airport. That would be the true test. We'd either be lost in the vast crowd, or they're so new and advanced we'd be spotted immediately, but we won't know for sure until we're out of Shanghai."

"We just may get to take that test," Chase said, hoping to be wrong.

They were flying straight into the dragon's mouth. The MSS may well have already identified them and be watching, tracking, waiting . . .

"We're entering the land of mass surveillance and the kingdom of facial recognition," Wen said as they arrived at Shanghai Pudong International Airport—the world's ninth busiest.

They sailed through customs without so much as a second glance from the officials. Wen's passport showed her as being Canadian, from Vancouver, a city with a large population of first and second generation Chinese. Chase's American passport had a different name, and passed the facial recognition scan. Both claimed the reason for their visit to China was for business, importing toys.

"So far so good," Chase said again. "Hope it goes this well throughout China."

Wen smiled, as if that were a silly notion.

Chase and Wen would have to continuously reapply

their vIDs masks to thwart the nearly one billion facial recognition cameras throughout China. Those same cameras made it too risky for Mei Lein to meet their flight, but she'd sent one of her most trusted people, Angúo—a skinny, twenty-something man—who acted as though he were meeting royalty, particularly Wen, who was a mythical-like figure in the Chinese section of The Cause. She was a legend in China's tight WOLF community, a woman who had been a top MSS agent, and now no longer existed. Someone who, until that moment, Angúo could not have been sure had ever existed. He'd so badly wanted to believe she was real, but couldn't help but doubt something that impossible.

"I am honored," Angúo said in an understated manner. "Thank you for coming to help with this problem. And . . . I'm sorry about your sister."

Wen stared at him a moment, then realized he must have known her sister. She thanked him for meeting them and introduced Chase.

"I'm sorry. We must go in the trucks," Angúo said, switching to English in deference to Chase.

The three of them got into the back of a cramped delivery truck. An hour later, they pulled into a loading dock and exited the truck. Several members of WOLF that Wen recognized were waiting, all people who had helped get her out, but Mei Lein was still not there. They hugged. One of the men cried as he held Wen. Some of them tried to talk, all at the same time. Wen was not just a myth, she was a savior.

They'd known her when she'd first come to The Cause. She had gotten out, and stayed out. Some of them wanted to be like her, but lacked the abilities to erase their identities.

Others wanted to stay and help liberate China, and then the world.

"Where is Mei Lein?" Wen asked in English.

"She coming," the man who had cried said. "It take long time. But she come."

"Are we staying here?" Wen asked, motioning to the warehouse.

One of the women laughed. "No, no, no. We have much farther to go tonight. You sleep in the car."

Chase closed his eyes. It was always difficult for him to sleep in vehicles, but they would be driving all night, so he would try. However, with the enormity of what they had to do and the mounting dangers closing in, sleep did not come easily as the Baojun 730 minivan sped through the night.

Chapter Thirteen

By morning, the vehicle carrying Chase and Wen had reached Tainjin. Soon they were taken to a modest house where Mei Lein was waiting. She updated them during a simple traditional breakfast of Jian Bing, tofu pudding, and tea.

Chase asked if they were certain that the government was sponsoring Mìng Rénshēng, since Chinese officials denied He Jiankui's twin embryo experiment had been sanctioned.

"It may be different in America," Mei Lein said, "but in China, nothing can happen without the government. You can be sure that the very top of the government knows about this, and that they are definitely controlling Mìng Rénshēng."

The man who'd cried seemed to know the most about the program, at least from a practical point, since he worked in the medical field. "They are trying to make new people, people the way they want. Smarter, stronger, taller." He smiled as he stretched up his hands more than a foot above

Chase's six-foot frame. "They want them to be super healthy, to live for long, long time."

"We had someone on the inside," Mei Lein began. "She came to us once she saw what they did. Three weeks ago, in a secret lab near Sichuan, part of Míng Rénshēng, a scientist successfully altered human DNA to improve intelligence in a living subject, a twenty-four-year old man." This small-boned, forty-something woman, her delicate fingers pouring tea, did not hide her strength, apparent in the way she carried her shoulders, obviously from years of martial arts and discipline. Yet a fatigue graced every last word, and a slight nod with softened eyes made Wen instantly know the pain she suffered from withstanding her country's atrocities.

"What happened?" Chase asked, suddenly no longer hungry as the implications of what the Chinese had done overwhelmed his tired mind. *A million years of human evolution altered in a blink.*

"The man's intelligence tested off the charts. It was disturbingly high, the woman told us. He shocked the doctors and scientists who had pioneered the procedure."

"It must have been incredibly complex," Wen said.

"Yes. I do not understand it myself," Mei Lein admitted. "Something like making a trillion copies and training the body to accept the change through a virus of some kind. That is why it is much, much easier to work on embryos that multiply themselves."

"Where is the man with super intelligence now?" Chase asked.

"Dead," Mei Lein replied. She looked out the window. A few leaves rustled in a cool breeze. "Apparently, three days after the procedure, the man himself predicted he would not live more than a few more days. He died sixteen hours later."

"When they altered the genes responsible for intelligence, it affected something else," Chase said.

"Exactly."

"I'd like to speak with the woman who told you this."

Angúo and Mei Lein exchanged a concerned glance.

"She is also dead," Mei Lein said sadly. "We do not know if they found out that she talked, or if the MSS executed everyone involved with the event."

Chase looked at Wen. She nodded slightly, confirming the MSS would do such a thing.

"The top scientists may have been spared and moved to another facility," Mei Lein said. "It is hard to know."

"They want to rule the world," Angúo said. He laid out the network of labs and gave them a list of the locations. He had a hyper energy, fidgeting around them as they looked at the specs. "We don't know where they all are, but this is most of them, and the most important one is BioCheng, just outside Beijing."

"If it's near Beijing, then we need to get in there. Why did we come all the way here?" Chase asked.

Angúo looked at Mei Lein, a confused expression on his face. "You cannot break into BioCheng," Mei Lein said.

"Why not?"

"It is impossible," Angúo said. "They are under MSS protection." He looked at Wen. "The security is all the best, every advanced technology. There is no way in."

"He is right," Wen said. "No MSS-Priority facility has ever been breached."

"What about hacking?" Chase asked.

"No," Mei Lein confirmed what he already knew. "The Míng Rénshēng labs and research centers are not on any networks."

"How do they share data then?" he asked, looking at the list of all the different locations spread across China.

"Couriers," Angúo said.

"Couriers?" Chase echoed. "They use *actual* humans to move the data?"

"Yes."

"Then that's our way in," Chase said.

"It won't be that easy," Wen said.

The man who had cried burst into the room. "Mei Lein," he said breathlessly, "we have to go! The authorities are coming!"

"I thought this was a safe house," Chase said as they all rushed to the garage.

"No house is safe," Mei Lein said. "Not since Sky Net."

Chapter Fourteen

Chase knew that China's "Sky Net" system's real name was "Pingan Chengshi", yet most Chinese citizens referred to it still as its English name, after the fictional artificial neural network of the Terminator movies. China's version, not yet as dangerous or powerful, was no less creepy. It operated real-time video surveillance, utilizing the most advanced AI facial recognition, and not only identified people, but also immediately provided the official viewer details on the subject such as age, sex, home address, workplace, social score, known associates, and more.

Chase, Wen, Mei Lein, and Angúo hurried into a van. The driver sped away while two vehicles took the other WOLF members in the opposite direction.

"Always running," Mei Lein said to Wen, and patted her knee. "It's good to see you, even under these circumstances."

"Yes," Wen said. Her life of freedom sometimes felt more trapped than before, but being back in China reminded her that she had done the right thing by fleeing the MSS.

"We need to get into BioCheng," Chase said, "and then we can leave."

"What about Yĭn Huāshù?" Angúo asked.

Mei Lein shook her head.

"What's Yĭn Huāshù?" Chase asked.

"*No*," Mei Lein said firmly.

Chase looked at Wen. "What does Yĭn Huāshù mean?"

"Hidden flowers," Wen said. "What is this, Mei?"

"It is *not* important."

"No secrets," Wen said, her words laced with anger toward her close friend. So much had happened in China since she'd fled. Had their trust been lost?

"It is a distraction."

"We should tell them," Angúo said. "It is part of this."

"No one even knows if the stories are true."

"We have risked Wen's life, and my life," Chase insisted. "You must tell us everything."

Mei Lein looked out the window as they crossed a suspension bridge leading into the city. She nodded at Angúo.

"Wait," she cut in. "Wen, this is a painful wound, not scarred over for me." She turned and wiped away tears. "Do not condemn me for wanting to keep silent." This was said in her native language.

Wen grabbed her hand, and nodded.

"Seven or eight years ago," Angúo began, "the scientists in our government began working on embryos, to make the children grow up the way they wanted. They . . . experimented."

"And the children were born?" Chase asked.

"Yes."

"My God. Six or seven years ago?"

"Yes."

"How many?"

"Maybe dozens."

"But we don't really know how many," Mei Lein warned.

"And they are alive?" Chase asked.

"We believe they might be," Angúo said.

"There are rumors," Mei Lein added.

"There are many stories that they are alive," Angúo continued. "Many stories about the hidden flowers."

"Yǐn Huāshù," Wen said. "Why do you call these children that?"

"They are children, after all," Angúo said. "No matter how they were made, and what they have been subjected to in the government's Mìng Rénshēng experiments, they are still innocent, like flowers, hidden from the world."

"What do you know about them? Are they okay?" Chase asked.

"There are many stories that the children have . . . abilities . . ."

"They're smarter and stronger?" Chase asked.

"Yes, but maybe other things. Special abilities," Angúo said. "They can do things that normal people cannot."

"We have heard that the children are different," Mei Lein clarified. "Some appear normal, some do not. They are, in some ways, better, and in other ways worse. They are experiments."

"These children, the hidden flowers, they would show what has happened, prove what they have been doing with the Mìng Rénshēng program," Chase said.

"Exactly," Mei Lein said. "That is why if they ever did

exist, they are surely dead now. The government would not be so foolish to leave such incriminating evidence alive."

"Unless they needed them," Wen said.

"Why would they?" Mei Lein asked, strength returning to her voice.

Wen shrugged. "Why are there rumors of them, if they never were?"

"Where are they?" Chase asked Angúo.

"You have to understand," Angúo began. "No one knows for sure *if* this happened, and if it did, no one knows if the children lived, and if they did, we do not know where they are."

"We must find them," Chase said, ignoring the first two parts of Angúo's statement. "There must be a way to find out where the Yīn Huāshù are." He looked at each of them in the van, bumping along, with a fierceness that silenced even Wen.

Angúo looked at Mei Lein, then back to Chase. "There might be a way."

Chapter Fifteen

Angúo explained that, *possibly*, they could locate the facility using the list of labs and overlaying satellite images. "If the hidden flowers are being held together in one place, there will be 'tracks'," Angúo explained. "The great disadvantage of being in the most monitored country on earth is that those same surveillance videos and images can also be used against the government."

"Sky Net flipped upside down," Wen said.

"Exactly."

Wen believed that The Astronaut could get into the system, but they would need more help, serious help, retrieving the spy satellite's data.

After the driver dropped them off in a parking garage, Chase, Wen, and Angúo took an elevator to a small office. It wasn't safe for Mei Lein, who was on a watch list, to be with them. Wen used the special encrypted and untraceable phone that the Astronaut had supplied them with and contacted him. At the same time, Chase called in the big guns, grateful that is was morning in the States.

Tess Federgreen was head of Corporate Intelligence Security Section. "CISS," perhaps the most secret division within the US intelligence community, had been formed as a joint operation of the CIA, NSA, and FBI, its mandate: to prevent war between corporations.

"Chase Malone, alive and in . . . China?" Tess said checking the screen as she took the call in her private office in the nondescript CISS headquarters building in Vienna, Virginia. "Please tell me you aren't being held prisoner, and that you weren't foolish enough to take Wen back to China."

"No, and yes," Chase said. "We need your help."

"I'm sure you do, but *China?*"

Tess, having risen through the ranks of the NSA, possessed an impressive list of Washington contacts, and knew more DC secrets than most. She'd been with CISS from the beginning, after years as a highly decorated CIA official. The ultra-classified division had been formed after a World Economic Forum report showed that only thirty-one of the top one hundred global economic entities were countries, with the other sixty-nine being corporations. The shocking trend, expected to continue, meant that in the next fifteen years, ninety-five conglomerates would dominate the list, with only five countries remaining. A highly classified joint CIA and NSA study concluded that a shift from nation states to corporate states made the likelihood of major conflicts, or "wars," erupting between companies, or corporations and countries, highly probable as the world entered a new phase of decentralized power. CISS had been created to keep the peace, and to make sure US interests were prioritized.

"We're here because of Míng Rénshēng."

Tess didn't respond for a moment. "Chase, I'm disappointed with you. However important you think it is to be in China, the two of you are in more danger than you can imagine." Silver studded, ornately designed cowboy boots rested on the edge of her desk, where she nursed a mug of hot mocha coffee. If she couldn't be swing dancing, then at least she could wear her hand-cut Taos artist boots, hidden under dark, sleek business slacks.

"We can handle ourselves."

"I admit you often surprise me, but Wen understands the capabilities and tactics of the MSS more than any of us. They. Will. Find. You." Tess's hard exterior unleashed one weakness other than dancing in some smoky Taos cabaret—Pueblo jewelry. A turquoise bracelet lazily hung, sort of like Buddha beads, where she'd move it around and around her wrist. It kept her mind focused.

Chase pushed forward, ignoring her warning. "I need some data."

"I wish you'd checked with me *before* you went there."

"Sorry we disappointed you," Chase said sarcastically, "but we weren't asking permission to be here."

"You forget my promise to Flint," Tess said, referring to Chase's former head of security, who'd had a longtime personal relationship with Tess. In his dying moments, he'd asked Tess to promise to keep Chase safe.

"Forget that," Chase said. "I absolve you of your commitment."

"I wish it were that easy," Tess said, removing her booted feet from her desk and planting them firmly on the floor. She moved deft fingers over several keyboards. "But it's not your place to release me from that promise, and, contrary to what you believe, I *do* care about you and Wen."

Nice to hear, and I hope that's true," Chase said. "While I'd love to continue chatting about old times, I'm afraid we've got a bit of a deadline here, and were not exactly calling from home, so . . . "

"How can I help?" Tess asked, tying back her long brown hair, which was just as often blonde, red, or a variety of shades. She'd become the most powerful woman in the intelligence business by anticipating every angle of a situation. Her years of experience, and quick, chess-champion's mind, usually gave Tess the advantage. She stared into split screens, one showing Chase and Wen's current location, the other rolling with facts about the Mìng Rénshēng program.

"Mìng Rénshēng is a government-sponsored network of scientists who are manipulating human genes."

"Interesting," Tess responded coolly, as if the name hardly mattered to her at all. However, over the last few months, it had become CISS's highest priority. She could hardly believe that Chase and Wen had somehow gotten involved in the dangerous arms race, something that posed a greater risk to society than even the height of the nuclear Cold War. "You're saying this goes beyond He Jiankui's twin embryo stunt?"

"Way beyond. They have dozens of research centers."

Tess looked at the list on her screen. "Really?"

"They've been at this for at least six years."

"How do you know that?" The information CISS had went back only four and a half years. She'd recently given a talk to the director of national intelligence, the heads of all seventeen national intelligence agencies, and the president of the United States, about the risks posed by Mìng Rénshēng. As far back as the Obama administration, CRISPR had been declared a weapon of mass destruction by then intelligence chief, James Clapper, but even so, in the passing years, and since China's botched announcement that it had modified embryos of the twin girls, almost everyone underestimated the dangers. In her presentation, Tess had proclaimed, "The complexities of CRISPR and the world-leading secret Míng Rénshēng program pose a threat unlike anything humanity has faced before, and, indeed, combine the elements of every threat we have seen before. Every single one. Not only are all of our enemies pursuing this technology, but enemies we don't know yet are going to use it for horrifying purposes. It is cheap and easy to obtain, and its ramifications are beyond imagining. They can unleash bioweapons in the form of humans, and on a scale never before seen. They can create genetic weapons and viruses to target specific populations . . . "

"We have sources," Chase said.

"You need to get out of there," Tess replied in a deadly sounding whisper.

"Why?"

"Because I don't want you starting World War Three."

Chapter Sixteen

The emergency national security meeting, which Tess had chaired, had been convened three days earlier after a serious data breach against the three top consumer genetic testing companies for ancestry, health, and DNA. In spite of rigorous security measures, the sites had been hacked. The same day, although still not publicly disclosed, the FBI's own DNA database had also been compromised. All of the attacks were believed to have originated from China.

"This data will allow China to target specific populations," Tess explained to Chase. "The threats are significant. The Chinese are gambling with the future, and with those high stakes, they won't hesitate to kill you both."

"I know," Chase replied dryly.

"No, you don't. They will hunt you every hour until they have you."

"You can help us or not," Chase said, continuing to ignore her warnings. "I'm trying to make sure our list of facilities in the program is complete. I've just sent you what we have on the network of scientific research centers."

Tess immediately knew what he was referring to. She quickly matched the list to what the CIA had, and sent him back a document detailing six more places he didn't have.

Chase showed it to Angúo, who, after consulting a computer, shook his head.

"That's a big deal Tess. Thanks."

"Happy to help," she said, suddenly sounding too nice. "Need anything else?"

"Actually, I do. We're looking for a place that they might have kept CRISPR test subjects."

Tess could not hide her surprise as she stumbled over her response. "Wh . . . what? *Living* subjects?"

"Yes."

"You're referring to the twin girls that were born HIV resistant? He Jiankui's experiment?"

"No."

"I didn't think so," Tess said. "So there are more?"

"Yes." Chase didn't want to say too much, but needed her help in finding them.

"How many?"

"Dozens. Maybe more. Maybe a lot more."

She gasped audibly. Tess, inside Secure, a room within CISS Mission Control where she could not be overheard, leaned against a wall and closed her eyes for a moment. Her job had just gotten harder, the problem and threat much more complex. "What are you looking for?"

"We need satellite access. We've only heard . . . If we can backtrack from the other facilities on the list . . . "

Tess's mind was already racing ahead. The US had incredibly comprehensive data on China. Their programs could slice and dice the seemingly endless information obtained through time satellite images and cyber spying to show construction, transfers, and movements going back years. Previously, it would have taken analysts months or years to sort through the material to find patterns and reach conclusions. However, with machine learning and artificial intelligence, including algorithms created by Chase, with the right inputs, they could process it in a matter of hours.

"I'll see what I can do," Tess said. "I'll need a little time."

"Thanks." Chase could almost calculate how long it would take. Tess was constantly trying to avoid wars, confrontations of all sizes and types. He didn't trust her, couldn't stand her, yet he liked knowing her. *Tess is like the brilliant professor who no one can stand, yet you know she's teaching you things. You know you need her,* he thought as he prepared to end the call.

"What are you *really* doing there?" she suddenly asked.

"Marrying Wen," he toyed.

She choked on a gulp of mocha. "*Seriously?*"

"Trying to *stop them*, Tess," Chase said quietly.

"That's not *your* job—but marrying Wen is!"

"It's everybody's job."

Tess, still leaning against a console in Secure, looked through the one-way glass wall into Mission Control, where dozens of people were working on the same problem as Chase. She nodded silently, even though he couldn't see her. She understood why he was risking everything and why Wen had put her life on the line to go back to China. She thought of Flint Jones and hadn't understood why he'd asked her to protect Chase. Now she wondered if he'd known more. Tess didn't believe in fate or destiny—at least she told herself she didn't—yet she couldn't help but ponder the possibility that she and Chase were locked together in some crazy twist of fate, their destinies to help each other, and was it somehow possible that Flint understood that.

"I can't send any helicopters to help. There'll be no IT-Squads to bail you out," Tess said, referring to the elite CISS teams that had already saved Chase and Wen more than once. "China is pretty much the most unreachable spot on earth for us—at least as far as boots on the ground"

"Then it's a good thing we're here," Chase said, looking at Wen.

"Yes, it is," she admitted. "Check back with me in a few hours. I'll see if I can track down your Frankenkids. Meanwhile, remember we don't want a war."

Chapter Seventeen

The train streaked through the countryside at more than two-hundred miles per hour, the scenery a blur of greens and beiges. Chase didn't like the mission. Too many people onboard, nowhere to run, cameras—those damned cameras were everywhere. They still hadn't heard back from Tess, and it had been almost six hours.

"Should we take him now?" Chase asked.

"I'm going to talk to him," Wen said.

Chase looked at her questioningly.

"He's just a courier," she said. "He shouldn't have to die for this."

Chase nodded reluctantly. He didn't want anyone to die, yet knew that if they allowed the wrong person to live, it might result in his or Wen's death. "Okay, but remember, the courier is moving the seeds of destruction for humanity."

"He probably doesn't know that."

If the conversation doesn't go well, Wen will resort to more prac-

tical means of obtaining the data package, Chase thought. The MSS data packages were known as suicide-drives, because the order was to die protecting them.

"If you don't need any help, I'm gonna work on the cameras," Chase said.

Wen resisted the urge to look up, still barely trusting the vIDs spray to protect them from the facial recognition gauntlet. She also decided not to warn him to be careful, not to get caught—things a wife or girlfriend would say—but traveling through enemy territory at two hundred and thirty miles per hour, seeking to intercept critical secret information belonging to the most dangerous regime on the planet, meant they were not lovers at that moment. Just two agents on a mission. She touched his hand, their eyes locked. Nothing needed to be said. Chase disappeared out the back of the car. Wen walked the other direction.

She stopped at the seat across from the courier and asked in Mandarin if the seat was taken. He looked up from his newspaper and appeared nervous. Then, seeing she was a pretty woman, he shook his head and indicated for her to sit.

"The train is not too crowded," Wen said, knowing the man had purposely sat in the back of the half empty car.

The man nodded and smiled. "No."

"I've just come from Beijing. It's a beautiful day there."

"Yes," the courier said, keeping his responses short and polite, not wanting to stand out, and definitely not wishing to encourage further conversation. He went behind his newspaper again.

"Did you also come from Beijing?"

He paused for a moment, perhaps debating whether to answer, or telling her he didn't wish to talk. Finally, he replied, "Yes."

"And where are you going?"

He named a town that wasn't too far, but she could tell immediately that he was lying.

"If I cannot trust you," she said firmly, "then I will have to kill you."

The man looked up, and before he could get his gun, Wen grabbed his hand and broke at least three of his fingers.

He managed to muffle an agonized moan, though no one was close enough to hear it anyway. Wen showed him her Glock 19 pistol, and glared in a way that he understood he would dare not move again. "I don't need the gun," she said, continuing to hold his stare. "And I don't want to use it."

"What do you want?" he asked, each word a gasp, his injured hand trembling.

"I'd like to save your life. Tell me your name."

"Bai," he said reluctantly, sweat forming on his sallow face.

"I know that you were at BioCheng today, and I know what you have. I want it."

"You are mistaken."

"Next lie is your last," Wen said. "Understand?"

He nodded weakly.

"I want the suicide-drive."

"You can have it."

"Thank you, but it is no good to me without the code, and without that code I will have to kill you. Do you know what is inside the package?"

"I have an idea. I will be killed if I give it to you, and not from your hands."

"Possibly. Do you have an idea? Because you look like a nice man." She pointed to his wedding ring. "Children?"

He didn't answer. She knew he wasn't answering because he did have children and wanted to protect them from whatever wrath she might be planning to inflict on his family.

"I will not hurt them, except as much as your death will bring pain on them, but we do not have to do this. The suicide-drive contains information on editing genes, altering the trajectory of evolution. This is very dangerous information that can cause great harm to humanity." She could tell by his face that he wasn't listening to the details of the contents, rather contemplating his fate. She squeezed his broken hand. He reeled back and cried out in pain.

"What I'm saying is important," Wen said in a sharp whisper. "How long have you been doing this job? Has anybody ever tried to take a package from you? No. That is because this one is different. This one will cause mass destruction, massive loss of life. You do not want this."

He shook his head, sweating in fear and pain.

"You give me the code, I will not kill you."

"How do I know?"

She gave him a trusting glance. He studied her face. "You know," she said firmly, but with a look of compassion that showed she understood his dilemma.

He could see this. He sensed that she had been in a position like his. She conveyed as much with her eyes.

"But how will I explain it? They will kill me!" They both knew his cooperation would mean execution.

"Because the code is not foolproof, and they know this. They understand that we can get in, but it will take time. I don't have that kind of time. That's why you must give it to me." She touched his other hand gently. "You *need* to do this."

The courier spoke slowly, reciting thirty-two digits. She slid the suicide-drive into a cellphone-sized computer and punched in the code.

Chapter Eighteen

Inside Minister Li's private office, a wall of large color photographs chronicled China's tremendous engineering feats, including the Great Wall, Three Gorges Dam, the Qinghai-Tibet Railway, Shanghai Tower, and the world's longest High-Speed Railway with the fastest bullet trains. Li believed China could do anything, and that it had been, for thousands of years, destined to lead the world. However, his beloved country now faced a critical challenge—would it overreach too soon?

He pushed a concealed button in his desk. The picture wall slid away to reveal an adjoining room containing a futuristic-looking command console.

Li stepped inside, immediately absorbing the many images and data feeds displayed on the room's rows of monitors. Within that unique space, he could view live feed satellite footage, China's facial recognition system, and access Ghost Dragon—China's ultra-advanced spy network.

The wall generally remained closed, but Míng Rénshēng meant it would now stay open indefinitely. Ever since the foolish decision to test the world with He Jiankui's twin embryos, things had been worsening. A leak from a woman who worked on the super-intelligence part of the project spoiled what should have been a cause for great pride. Although the edited-man died less than eighty-eight hours after the procedure, it had been successful, and China was far ahead of the rest of the world.

That unauthorized disclosure had been dealt with swiftly, the leaker killed, yet damaging repercussions from her crime had unearthed a larger internal problem.

Li's lieutenant, Shen, appeared behind him.

"The arrests have begun," he told his boss.

"Not too many," Li replied, still watching the screens, discreetly chewing dried, salted plums.

"Just as we discussed. Only enough to let them know we are coming."

"Good. Our best interrogators."

"Of course," Shen assured him. Li's plan had been to shake up the dissident groups so they would make mistakes. At the same time, they would torture the ones they arrested to gain more internal intelligence on the groups. Li knew that in a county with one and a half billion people, there were plenty of malcontents. The MSS was currently monitoring more than six thousand secret opposition groups. Government estimates put the problem in the millions of people, more than two thirds of whom were students and young people. Religious organizations were another issue; the Communist Party dealt with them by closing churches and jailing pastors. They were easier to handle because of their being out in the open. The other groups were the real threat.

"I want the leaders of any group opposed to our science

initiatives." The minister turned to face Shen. "Understood?"

"Please do not imply I would not carry out your order," Shen said.

"I am not," Li said, moving his stare back to the monitors, but they both knew it was a warning.

Chase returned to the train car just as they were slowing to pull into a station. Wen handed him the suicide drive.

"All the cameras in this section have been disabled, our presence erased." It had taken some doing, but the Astronaut had located the schematics. "Thank goodness I had my multi-tool." He smiled.

"You see?" Wen said to the courier. "No one will know."

As soon as they were off the train, Wen made a point of showing the cameras that the courier was a hostile prisoner. She pushed him around and held a gun to his back.

Half a minute later, Chase exited through another door. They went separately so the cameras wouldn't tag them as a couple.

Wen escorted the courier behind a building. "I'm going to have to shoot you," she told him. "So they won't kill you."

He nodded.

"It'll have to be in the stomach."

The courier looked at her with a desperate expression.

"If I don't, they'll know it was a setup. Don't worry, I've been trained in anatomy . . . and shooting. I won't hit anything vital." She handed him the gun she'd taken from him on the train.

"Fire it into the air, so there'll be powder on your hand."

She gave him a warning glance. "If you shoot me, I'll kill you."

He said nothing, simply closed his eyes and aimed at the sky.

"Good luck, Bai," she whispered.

He did as he was told, and at the same instant, she shot him. It was a good hit. But she was already sprinting away before he hit the ground. Seconds later, she caught up to Chase, knowing, after passing six different cameras, that they were already being pursued.

Chapter Nineteen

Chase and Wen jogged into a large commuter parking lot.

"Are you okay?" he asked while scoping out cars.

"Fine."

Chase understood "fine" didn't actually *mean* fine, but it also didn't necessarily mean *not* fine. It really meant *let's talk about this after we steal the car and get away from here.*

The lot was divided into sections, with the area farthest from the station for longer-term parking. "Those will give us a better chance," Chase said, knowing the owners might not be around so soon to report them stolen.

"The cameras will report us," Wen said.

"They're mostly only Chinese-made vehicles. Not my favorite," Chase said, at the same time as sirens began to blare. A light gray Wuling Hongguang van was the closest choice. They thought it might blend in well. Once on the road, Chase gauged Wen's state of mind again. "That went as well as could be expected."

"Duì," Wen absently confirmed in her native Mandarin.

"Do you think the MSS will believe the courier didn't cooperate?"

"It depends on who questions him," Wen said, checking the side mirror. "If I were interrogating him, I would know. My former supervisor, Rong Lo, would also have found his lie. However, there are many MSS agents who would not see the deceit, or would just let it go, willing to ignore the obvious."

"What's the obvious?" Chase asked, passing a slow car.

"That he is still alive."

Chase nodded. He could sense the regret in her voice. Even though she had spared the man, the odds were he would still die because of them.

"We had to get this information," Chase said. "Sometimes our objectives require people to get hurt who aren't necessarily trying to kill us. They're still part of the system that is inevitably trying to hurt us or others."

"Is that how you justify it?" Her voice came out louder than she wanted.

"It's how I try, because I don't know what else to do," Chase said calmly, checking the navigation system, not sure where they were heading other than attempting to put distance between them and the train station. "I believe in our cause, that it must be done, and that we're doing it as carefully as possible."

Wen made a noise that sounded like an angry sigh, but he wasn't sure. She was concentrating on reading the suicide drive on their handheld computer.

"We took a greater risk not killing the courier. Ultimately, is that the right thing to do? Will we be forced to kill more people later by leaving a trail?"

"Maybe," Wen said. "We have a two hour drive." She

gave him the name of the town. "It would've taken us twenty minutes on the train."

Two hours was precious time. Every minute they remained in China was a minute closer to their deaths. They both knew this. Wen especially could feel the clock ticking like a tightening noose around her neck. But staying on the train would've been too dangerous. They certainly would've been caught. Yet driving a stolen vehicle on a major Chinese highway in broad daylight was a whole other kind of risk.

"We need to look for a place to find another car," Chase said. "It won't take them long, checking the cameras around the commuter lot, to determine which vehicle we stole."

"Seems to be a good-sized town not too far ahead," Wen said, checking the navigation system.

"Where are we going?"

"The facility that created the super-intelligent man."

"How are we going to get in?" Chase asked, pleased that their abduction of the courier had yielded such valuable data.

They took the exit and found a parking lot behind a small office building, figuring they'd have until the end of the workday before a car was discovered missing. Chase approached the lot on foot while Wen abandoned the van in an underground parking garage. Soon they were back on the highway in a brand new silver sedan, manufactured by a company called **"Geely,"** which Wen assured him meant *lucky* in Mandarin.

"I'll take all the luck we can get!" Chase said. Traffic was moderate.

"At this rate, we should be at the research facility in about ninety minutes," Wen said, glancing at the nav-screen before returning her concentration to the rest of the data from the courier.

Almost half an hour later, Chase checked the rearview mirror and cussed.

Wen turned around in her seat and groaned at the sight of a police car with flashing lights zooming toward them.

Chapter Twenty

The police car closed in quickly. Chase, always ready to don his race car helmet and push the limits of physics, instead felt a lump in his throat. In China, the rules were different. Even as he had that thought, they passed under a bank of highway cameras.

"I don't think we have a chance to outrun them in this traffic," Wen said.

"We don't have a chance to outrun them in this rinky-dink Geely," Chase said. "And this car sure doesn't seem very lucky."

"If we pull over, we're as good as dead."

"There's an exit up ahead," Chase said.

"You just said we couldn't outrun him."

"Let's just get him into a more secluded location."

Wen knew what he was thinking, and realized they might have a chance, but was saddened for a moment at the thought of killing a police officer who was just doing his job, who had no idea of the trouble he was about to pull over.

The police cruiser, lights still flashing, followed them off the exit ramp. Chase stopped on the shoulder beneath the underpass.

"Quick, trade places," Wen said, sliding on top of him. Chase struggled to maneuver into the passenger seat. "Let me do the talking." She winked.

Chase, who only spoke a dozen words of Mandarin, had no intention of trying to do any of the talking. He concealed a gun inside his jacket. Wen had hers under her legs. "Do you have a plan?" he muttered as the officer walked cautiously up to their vehicle, but no more so than he might've on a routine stop—or at least that's how Chase assessed the situation.

"I might," she said.

Chase knew she always had a plan, this time he just couldn't figure out what it was. "Care to let me in on it?"

The officer was only a few feet from her window. Chase was grateful the man was alone, although he could have easily already radioed in their plate number. It still seemed possible that no one could connect Chase and Wen to the vehicle, at least not yet.

"I'm going to take him as soon as he asks me to step out of the car," Wen whispered, as she lowered her window.

The officer appeared at the side of the car and asked her something in Mandarin. Chase thought he looked nice enough, almost friendly. *Can't be much older than me.* Chase spotted his wedding ring and wondered if he had any kids. He momentarily felt sorry for the man. It didn't matter how much training the cop had, or how many weapons—no single person was a match for Wen.

Chase assumed the officer was making a request for papers, but he didn't understand a word of it, nor of Wen's response. Suddenly, the policeman opened her door. Even though Chase knew where Wen's machine gun was and watched intently, he didn't understand how she stood up out of the car and shifted the weapon behind her back as she was standing.

The officer didn't see her gun until he was slammed into the side of the car with it shoved in his back. Chase jumped out as Wen disarmed the man and pushed him toward the back of the vehicle.

He followed them to the rear of the police cruiser. "Get his keys," Wen said to Chase. "Open the trunk." She gave the cop a forceful hit in his side and told him to get in the trunk. As he climbed in, she raised her gun. The policeman must have assumed she was going to kill him. Instead, she shot several holes in the trunk.

The officer crawled into the back of the trunk. Wen said a final few words in Mandarin, and then closed him in.

"What'd you say to him?" Chase asked as they rushed back to the Geely.

"I reminded him that we could have killed him, but we did not. And asked that he please do the same for us."

"Do you think it's smart to leave him?"

"Of course not. Leaving anyone alive is a horrible idea," Wen said. "It counters all my training and experience. Never leave a witness. Remove all threats, permanently. We are taught to kill, to destroy all obstacles."

They started the car and squealed away.

"But he doesn't need to die," Wen continued. "By the time someone finds him, we'll be long gone."

"Unless he radioed ahead," Chase said quietly.

"Yeah," she agreed. "If he did, we're dead."

Chapter Twenty-One

Wen checked the navigation system and told Chase to take a left, away from the highway.

"We need to stay off the main roads now."

"Are there such things as back roads around here?" Chase asked.

"Yes, but it's China," Wen said as Chase pulled around to pass another car. Chase knew what she meant. China—cameras everywhere, the definition of totalitarian state. Nowhere to hide. "Let's see where we're going." She brought up the GPS, half expecting to see police cars on the screen chasing them. Tracing the route, Wen began formulating a plan. She knew next to nothing about the facility where they were heading. However, the MSS had trained her for just such a situation. There were certain things every institution had in common, and those were the aspects on which she would create her plan.

"We'll need to switch vehicles again," Chase said. "As soon as possible."

Wen didn't respond.

"Hey, where are you?" Chase asked.

"Maybe I *should* have killed the courier, and the policeman," she said softly.

"We would be in even more danger if we had," Chase said.

"There is too much at risk," she said forcefully. "We cannot afford the luxury of feelings."

"Yes, we can," he said, touching her leg. "Besides, good karma is something we can use right now."

They didn't speak for several miles, until a vast city skyline appeared above the trees in front of them.

"Something's wrong," Chase said.

"What?" Wen spun around in her seat to look behind them.

"This city isn't on the GPS."

Wen zoomed in and out on the dashboard map, trying to find it.

"I don't know of a city here."

"I thought you were familiar with this part of the country?"

"We memorize every city and town." Wen checked the in-dash system. "Even if I had forgotten it, the GPS should have it."

"Maybe the system is wrong."

"If it's wrong, then maybe we're going to the wrong place."

"Or that city is not there at all." Chase compulsively checked the rearview mirror.

"We're not going back the way we came."

"Let's see if the Astronaut can find it. We don't want to be driving into a secret military installation," Chase said. "He should have some more information from the courier's data by now anyway."

"And still no word from Tess about the hidden flowers."

"Maybe they don't exist. But we know the man with super intelligence lived, and to learn more on that, we have to get information at the facility where they made him."

"I know," she said resignedly. "It's not going to be easy to get into a place like that. The MSS will have set up their security. They'll be monitoring."

"Getting in?" Chase asked, checking behind them again. "I'm more worried about getting *out*. But if we can pull it off, there should be enough data that we could leave the country immediately afterwards."

He noticed her sad expression.

"Hard for you?"

"China is my home, but I cannot stay. It is difficult to think of leaving again."

"I know."

"I'll worry about that later. Right now we need to focus on getting another vehicle, and finding out what city this is." She looked at her phone. "It's not connecting to the Astronaut."

"Could be why we haven't heard back from Tess, no international coverage here."

"Or they are onto us, blocking us . . . The MSS would do that. Just watch, see who we meet with, where we go, then pounce." She checked the sideview mirror again.

"Maybe he didn't call it in," Chase said, referring to the police officer.

"Maybe. But it won't take long before somebody finds him."

"Look at this," Chase said, as they entered an area that appeared to be modern commercial district. "Is it a holiday? Where is everybody?"

"Now I know why this city is out of place," Wen said, as Chase stopped at a red traffic light.

"Why, because we've entered another dimension and come out in the twilight zone?"

"Twilight zone?" she asked, unfamiliar with the reference.

"Never mind. What is this place? And please don't tell me it's a nuclear testing ground."

"It's a ghost city," Wen said matter-of-factly.

Chapter Twenty-Two

Minister Li watched the monitors in his private office. He took pride in the fact that China had such advanced technology, which afforded him a great deal of detail. Still, it was nowhere near the US CIA, NSA, and Pentagon capabilities. *However, one day*, he thought, *we will surpass the Americans.* And that was part of what he was working toward. In fact, ultimately surpassing the Americans represented his entire career.

Shen came in, after being cleared by Li's secretary. "We lost a courier," he said, as if announcing the death of a loved one.

"Where?" Li asked, knowing exactly what kind of courier Shen meant. He began switching through the monitors, searching for the system alert. Li had been concerned about the exposure to the Míng Rénshēng program by using physical carriers, but MSS experts had assured him it was safer than allowing the data onto hackable networks.

Shen told him the location. "He was abducted on a

train. They had some sort of information as to where he was traveling."

"The couriers, and their routes, are extremely guarded secrets," Li said, staring at the screens, still cycling through the monitors, trying to bring up the region in which the attack took place. "What happened? Was he killed?"

"No, just injured." The two men exchanged a knowing glance. The lieutenant voiced Li's suspicion. "Normally, he would have been killed as to not identify his attackers."

Li nodded.

Shen continued, "He's being questioned by our people right now. Perhaps they had no time to kill him, and this may be a break. He may be able to tell us something about who it was."

"How long does it take to kill a man . . . an instant." Li remained skeptical. "They would've killed him. He was in on it. I want him brought here."

"I'll see to it. There could be another explanation." Yet even as Shen uttered the words, he didn't believe them. Whoever had intercepted the courier was a professional. Just to obtain the information of his identity and route would've taken tremendous resources. Ming Rénshēng was the MSS's highest priority, and therefore those couriers' identities were ultra-protected. Li had recommended escorts, but it was decided that would bring too much attention to them. He now regretted that decision.

"I want four agents on every courier effective immediately. This could well be the start of a coordinated effort."

"Terrorist," Shen said.

"I'm not so sure," Li countered. "What was the courier carrying?"

"I'm waiting to hear from the director of BioCheng."

Li, not a patient man, wasn't used to having to wait for

information he needed. Typically calm and cool, his expression suddenly turned angry. "How dare anyone attack the state like this, within our own borders."

Shen nodded at his outrage.

"Dissidents," Li said. "This is more likely their work."

Shen wanted to agree with him, because terrorists would be a far more dangerous proposition not just for China, but for humanity. If it was a dissident, it would mean that somebody else had found out about the Míng Rénshēng program, and maybe they were trying to stop it. However, either scenario offered challenges to the MSS, and his sworn duty to protect the state.

"It's either somebody on the inside," Shen said, "or somebody working at the originating or destination lab."

"The destination lab doesn't get the data until the courier arrives, so that limits it to the originating lab, and if that's the case, there's only three people." Li continued turning over the puzzle in his mind—dissident or terrorist. The terrorist would've killed the courier. Even if there was no time, there would've been time for that. However, dissidents, of which the courier was somehow sympathetic to, or connected to through family, or some other means, would shoot the courier to protect him, to make it look like a legitimate attack.

"Where was he shot?" Li asked.

"Abdomen."

The minister sucked in a breath. "What's his condition?"

"Stable. He can talk."

That answer solidified it for Li. If the man had been in critical condition, he might've believed he had no inside knowledge, but stable and talking meant he was in on it somehow, or else he'd be dead.

"If the courier was on the inside, we have a bigger problem," Shen said, knowing what his boss was thinking.

"Don't start," Li said bitterly, letting his lieutenant know he was in no mood to hear more theories about the dangers of gene editing.

"You know it's dangerous, and this proves what I've been saying all along. There are people out there who want to use this science for nefarious reasons and harm."

"I will inform the President and the committee of the developments. They will draw the appropriate conclusions and decide on a course of action."

"But you know they're not going to stop the program unless you scare them. Informing them of the developments, the appropriate course of action, all of that just feeds the status quo, reinforcing the absence of risk. It could not be further from the truth." He flexed a fist, revealing ripped arm muscles, and punched his hand in a controlled movement.

"I'm not going to sensationalize this."

"You don't *have* to sensationalize it. Somebody just attacked a courier, in broad daylight, in the middle of China, and took some of our most classified secrets—secrets that have the capacity to alter the DNA and evolution of humanity. What's to sensationalize?"

They exchanged another tense glance. Although Li was the superior, and one of the most important men in China, he had learned to trust Shen's judgment. On no other matter had Shen ever disagreed with him. Shen's silence in their stare asked the unspoken question—could Li admit to himself that Shen might be completely right, because to do so would jeopardize his mission.

"I'm not asking you to do anything illegal or act against the state," Shen implored. "I'm only asking you to talk to the leadership and convince them they are on a perilous path."

"That is more difficult," Li said. The hierarchy of China's leadership did not like to be questioned, and certainly not if they didn't invite it.

"This is proof enough," Shen repeated. "This is the opening you need to talk to the President. I beg you not to squander it."

Chapter Twenty-Three

Chase looked at the massive silver and glass skyline. It seemed impossible that a place so expansive could really be devoid of people.

"China is so big that instead of having ghost towns, they have ghost *cities*?" he asked, looking around at the gleaming megalopolis that could have been Seattle or Austin—shiny skyscrapers, wide boulevards, miles of freshly built perfection. "This is a *huge* city. Where is everyone?" Chase asked again.

"They haven't moved in yet. China has three or four hundred million people expected to move from the rural areas to cities, and there's no room in Shanghai or Beijing, so many urban areas are already over-crowded. To solve the problem, the government has built dozens of these cities around the country, complete and ready, just waiting for people."

"You've gotta be kidding me. This is extraordinary!" Chase exclaimed. "Did it ever occur to them to start small, build a few buildings, let some people relocate, then do the rest in steps?"

"No. People would not want to come to a place with no other people. They want to move to the big city with lots of opportunities, so the government builds it all at once."

"If no one lives here, I'm not sure we're going to be able to switch cars."

"Actually, it may be the perfect place to find a *new* vehicle," Wen said, looking ahead, as if trying to locate a parking area. "The government has these places totally ready. Somewhere there should be lots full of vehicles. The shops should all be full of goods, just nothing perishable."

"So, you're saying no lunch?" He winked.

"I've got some energy bars."

"I was thinking fish and chips."

"Be thinking cars."

"Okay, where would *you* put the cars?" he muttered while scanning up a side street, hoping to see a big parking sign like they had in American cities. "How many people are they expecting?"

"Probably two million."

Chase shook his head. They continued driving and looking for parking lots. The traffic lights and electronic signs all functioned as if the town was occupied. Store fronts were set up, everything appeared normal—just no people. Chase felt as if they were in a post-apocalyptic movie and that at any moment zombies, or gangs of mutant survivors from some kind of nuclear holocaust, were going to surround them.

"What about those?" Chase asked, pointing to cameras on the utility poles. More were on buildings, concealed in the traffic lights . . .

Everywhere.

"It's China. The cameras work all the time."

"But there's no one here."

"They are monitored by AI, and they aren't looking for us, remember?" She tapped her face, indicating the spray-on vIDs.

"We don't even know if that still works," Chase said. "We should reapply."

"I don't think we can do it in the car. Let's go in there."

Chase pulled over to the side of the wide street and parked along the curb. They kept their faces low and headed to a department store entranceway.

"It's locked."

She smiled. "Of course it's locked. In America, do they leave stores unlocked when they're closed?" He looked at her as if her question were absurd while taking out his multitool. After nearly half a minute of watching Chase unsuccessfully try to work the lock, Wen opened her bag and pulled out a small kit, picked the padlock in less than a second, opened the door, and said, "Enter Sir," in Mandarin. "It's all about having the right tool," she said, running in after him.

"I almost had it," Chase said.

"Of course."

"I can't believe they actually have electricity that works."

"They do it all," Wen said, "but I don't think it's going along too well. People may never move here. Some cities have been vacant for a number of years."

"They can't get the urban planning and internal migration right, yet these same people believe they can correct and enhance evolution to make superhumans?" he said, half joking, and then adding in a deadly serious tone, "We've got to stop them."

"Over here," she said, pointing to a large, elaborate

dressing area that included leather sofas and a room full of mirrors. She took the vIDs applicator out of her pack and they took turns putting it on each other.

"Okay, now let's go car shopping," Chase said.

As they headed out, Chase stopped at a rack of leather jackets.

"What do you think of this for me?"

"We have enough trouble, let's not add stealing."

"You think after all we've done, they're going to arrest us for shoplifting? You think that's a real problem?"

"Leave the jacket," she said. "Karma."

They passed the jewelry counter. Chase turned back to her. "You sure? Those diamonds would look beautiful on you."

She smiled. "No thank you. And none of that's real anyway. In China, the real jewelry is kept locked up until the display pieces are chosen by the customer. In the glass cases, only synthetic diamonds and other gemstones catch the light, which would fool any nonexpert, even people who work in regular jewelry stores."

Once outside the main entrance, Chase got that dystopian feeling again. They were not alone.

Chapter Twenty-Four

Chase shivered as they pulled away from the curb and steered the car onto the big empty street. He absently stopped at a red light. Then, realizing there was no point, was about to pull through when he suddenly saw a camera and stopped again. "Maybe there's some kind of automated system that notifies authorities if someone violates a law," Chase said. "No need to risk alerting anyone."

A block later, he slowed, thinking there was a parking lot behind an ornate church, but there was not access. They had to leave the car and jog around the side street. "Nothing," Wen said, once they got behind the building.

Chase stopped next to a small graveyard adjoining the church. "None of the tombstones have any names or dates on them," Chase said.

"The government has thought of every detail to make it a real city."

"Or they're waiting for people to die."

Wen ignored him. She held out her arm. "Hear it?"

"What?" Chase asked, but he was used to her always

hearing things before him. At first he thought it was some crazy psychic sixth sense or something, but she had explained that the MSS put them through constant training to heighten their hearing and identify sounds barely perceptible in silence and also in otherwise multi-noise atmospheres. She already had her Glock out. They had left their submachine guns in the car.

"Helicopter." She lowered her stance and was moving rapidly toward the car. Chase, completely unarmed other than his multitool, moved more daringly, desperate to get the machine gun. He couldn't stand guns, but had learned to rely on them. As Wen often reminded him, "*You may not like guns, but you love life.*"

Now he heard it, the sound that permeated his nightmares. There always seemed to be people after them in helicopters.

They reached the car. Chase lunged in and grabbed a machine gun as if it were oxygen.

"That helicopter is leaving," Wen said.

"Maybe it was just a patrol?"

"An injured Courier robbed on a high-speed train, a police officer locked in the trunk of his car, two stolen vehicles in the area? You wildly underestimate the Chinese authorities, and especially the MSS. That helicopter dropped a team into the city. They're using the cameras, and probably satellites, to hunt us right now."

"Then let's go!"

"No car," Wen said. "That's the easiest way for them to find us. We're safer on foot." She grabbed their guns and pack.

"That car is our only way out of the city," he reminded her.

"Let's worry about surviving first, and transportation

later," Wen said, jogging back towards the department store. "Remember, somewhere in this city there are parking lots filled with vehicles. That's not going to be our problem."

"Okay, another dumb question," he yelled, following her. "Why are you heading back the way we came?"

"We're going to the department store."

"Did you change your mind about the jewelry?"

"The store has a security office," she said. "All major businesses in the newer cities have them, and with the right access, it will be linked to the security network and cameras for the entire city."

"But won't they see us go there on the very cameras we'll be using?"

"Don't worry, we're not staying long. Besides, they already know exactly where we are."

A few minutes later, Wen had located the security office, a wide room filled with large screens hung on painted, concrete-block walls. She powered on the surveillance system and large aluminum computer towers that routed the massive streams of video data. The first images were different views of the store. Working the keyboards as if she ran the office every day, Wen adjusted the settings so that the two entrances were permanently visible on one of the split screens so no one could sneak in on them.

As she cycled through the feeds, eventually Wen found the proper access sequence to bring up the entire city.

"How did you do that?"

"Educated guess," she said.

"Guess?"

"Not exactly. The default setting for most of the systems is one of three different codes. I figured since nobody is here yet, it was still set on default. The second one worked."

"Standard MSS training 101?" he asked.

She nodded, and began pulling up different views of the city. Once again, Chase was amazed at how large the ghost city was.

"There are hundreds and hundreds of buildings!" he said as the city flashed by. "Look at all the restaurants, furniture stores, grocery stores, theaters, bars, fitness centers, apartments, condos . . . there must be a hundred bike rental stations. Maybe we could bike out of town." He watched it all go by with an eerie sense that they really were in a surreal episode of the Twilight Zone. "Where is everybody?" he silently asked himself again, even though an inner part of him was screaming. It felt as if the world was spinning upside down. The sense that they were the last couple on earth returned. The unnerving thoughts made him dizzy.

The ghost city is like fast forwarding to what will happen if the Chinese destroy humanity by altering the evolutionary chain, he thought. *All the evidence of human civilization—the buildings, cars, planes, and battleships—all the* stuff *will still be here, but the people will be gone. The arrogant scientists will adjust the wrong gene and suddenly humanity will be wiped out as we succumb to something like pollen, or the common cold.*

"There!" Wen snapped, shattering the silence and bringing him back to the current crisis. She pointed to one of the many monitors. He looked up and all the strange feelings of isolation, the unsettled idea that they had survived the end of humanity, vanished when he saw the enemy. Eight heavily armed MSS agents, clad in black, were moving rapidly toward the department store.

Chapter Twenty-Five

Chase looked at the team of agents on the screen with a deep feeling of foreboding. Perhaps the thoughts that had been filling his head, their absolute isolation, or watching the eight approaching, made it seem worse, but he wasn't sure they were going to escape this time.

"How far away are they?" he asked.

"Looks like two blocks," Wen said, after a few keystrokes overlaid the map and distances of what was happening on that specific camera.

"Then we have time," Chase said, already moving toward the door.

"No, it's not just them. There are two more."

"Two more agents?"

"Two more *teams*. Eight agents each."

"How do you know?"

She looked away from the monitor for only a second to shoot him a look as if to say, *Why are you asking that question?* Then she answered anyway. "In this situation, standard

MSS protocol requires three teams. Twenty-four agents to overwhelm the two targets."

"We're the targets."

"Yes, honey." She smiled despite the danger at hand. "And they aren't amateurs."

"Where are the others?"

"Here's one. Half a block away. Here's the other, farther out."

"We should go while we can still get away."

"They won't let us leave the city. There's only one way out."

"Through twenty-four dead MSS agents?" Chase asked.

She nodded, her eyes sad and hard at the same time.

Chase watched the other team, two blocks away and closing in fast. The ones that were half a block away would be there any minute. "We've got to go."

The closest team disappeared from the monitor.

"We need to know where they are," she said, pointing to the monitors.

"They'll be in this room in a minute if we don't *leave*. I'd rather be alive and wondering about their whereabouts than be dead and know where they are."

"It's better to find them before they find us."

"Wen, seriously, let's get out of here."

"Where are you? Where *are* you?" Wen asked the monitors as she scanned, trying to pick them up again.

Chase pointed to one of the upper screens. "There!" He looked in horror at their location. "We couldn't find them because they're already in the building!"

"Now we go," Wen said.

Chase stole one last glance at the monitors—the farthest team was about a block away, and the second team was across the street.

"Where?" Chase hissed. "There's nowhere *to* go."

"Up." She rounded the corner and pushed through a door to the stairwell.

"What's up?"

"The roof."

"I assumed the roof," Chase barked. "Do we have a helicopter waiting?"

"I hope not. The only helicopter around here is MSS, and I'm not interested in going where they want to take us."

"Are you being this way because I left my gun in the car earlier?"

"I'm being this way because we've got twenty-four trained killers after us, and we've only got three guns."

"But the roof—how are we going to get *off* the roof?"

"I don't know yet, I haven't been up there. Maybe you can do something with your multi-tool."

She was flying effortlessly up the stairs. Chase had to work to stay with her.

"You saw the monitors. Going downstairs wasn't an option," she continued. "Security office is on the third floor, and the building is eight stories. They have a lot of ground to cover."

They burst out onto the roof. A gust of wind almost knocked them down. Chase, an experienced skyscraper climber from his days working with his brother Boone's San Francisco window washing business, surveyed the area. At the same time, he was applying his knowledge of engineering, trying to find any advantage in the coming battle. Wen also searched for defensive positions, areas where she could spring a trap, launch an offensive, do as much damage as possible, and take out a disproportionate number of the enemy. Neither one of them particularly liked what they saw. The tower, like many modern structures in China, had been designed in a sleek, minimalistic style, all gleaming glass and polished metal.

"What you think?" Chase asked, sounding a little too desperate.

Wen didn't answer.

Chase took a deep breath. Time was ticking away, and Wen's usual endless supply of escape plans might have finally dried up. He jogged around the outside perimeter of the roof. "We do have one option," he yelled back at her in the wind.

"*No,*" she shouted, realizing his idea.

"There's no choice. We have to jump!"

Chapter Twenty-Six

Chase and Wen stood side-by-side, looking over the edge of the eight-story department store tower. "That one's close enough," Chase said.

"No it's not," Wen said, looking at the building he'd pointed to—another silver tower nearly identical to theirs, except one story shorter. "It's definitely not close enough."

"We can make it," Chase said. "The wind is at our backs."

As with so many of the skyscrapers in China, this one was a beautiful statement, and together with the neighboring buildings, it cascaded like a staircase, forming a modern, abstract waterfall—each structure one floor lower than the next. The "waterfall" ended at a one-story center down the street.

"The distance between the buildings is probably *thirty* feet," Wen protested.

"If we get a running start . . . "

"That's still a tough jump," Wen said. "Almost impossible."

"*Almost*," Chase said. "If our lives depend on it, we can make it."

"They do."

"We need a running start."

"From the entire length of the roof," Wen said.

"But if we wait until they get up here—"

"They'll shoot us before we even get to the edge. We can't wait." She pointed to cameras. "The agents will be here soon. They know where we are. Then they'll know we're on the next building."

"I wasn't planning on staying on that one."

"You want to do *another* jump?"

"They'll shoot us if we don't."

"How many jumps do you want to do?"

Chase counted the buildings. "Just until we get to the bottom . . . looks like seven until we get to the last one, and then we still have to get to the ground. The first one is the hardest."

"They're all the same."

"Not true. With each one, the fall is a little less."

"I've got news for you, falling from an eight story building, falling from a six-story building, or falling from a four-story building, it's all the same if you're landing on *concrete*."

"We're not going to fall."

Wen nodded dubiously. "Then you're right. The longer we wait, the better, because otherwise they'll just get agents on the next roof to wait for us."

"Then we wait up until that point," Chase said.

"Up until that point," she agreed. Wen had been counting ever since she saw the agents in the monitors, estimating, keeping track of how long it would take for them to get to the roof, playing through every possible scenario based on her MSS training, experience, and the scale of the building. "They're in the stairs," Wen said. "Most likely on the fifth floor."

Chase looked around as if she had somehow found the bank of surveillance monitors on the roof, but there was nothing. "Ready?" They both stood like Olympic runners waiting for the starting gun.

"Sixth floor."

"When do you want to go?"

"Once they're on the seventh, which should . . . be . . . now!"

They took off running full speed towards the edge. They sprang off the final inch of steel as if their lives depended on it, as if there was some magic staircase waiting for them, as if the act of faith would be enough to propel them to the other side, to safety. Neither one looked down, both knowing the secret of athletes—focus on the finish line, never release the goal from your mind, never look away from where you want the ball to go. In this case, *they* were the ball, and they needed a perfect home-run knocked out of the park.

They flew through the empty air above the empty city they shared with only the twenty-four killers.

Eight of those killers, dressed in black, charged out of the glass-topped silvery hatch that concealed the stairwell entrance onto the roof of the building Chase and Wen had just left. Their guns swept the area in anticipation of shooting their prey. The MSS agents, collectively stunned to find no one on the roof, ran in all directions to the edges of the building.

"Over here!" one of the men shouted in Mandarin as he began firing at Chase and Wen.

Chase heard the first bullet zing past his head. It had

been too close, but bullets were the least of his worries as he sailed nearly one-hundred feet above the pavement and had yet to reach the other building. He judged the distance remaining—

We're not going to make it.

Chapter Twenty-Seven

Minister Li sat alone in front of his monitors, eating a bowl of peanuts and salted plums. He liked to shell peanuts while he watched interrogations. The first one bored him. A twenty-year-old man, who had already been kicked out of college, denied plotting against the state. The officer handling the case was not MSS, but that didn't matter. This "kid" had been picked up more than eight hundred miles from where Li sat.

The minister glanced at another screen, which contained a detail of the dissident's prior charges and a complete overview of his life. When it became apparent that the kid had nothing to offer, Li sent instructions to the regional judge to make sure he would sentence him to eighteen months in prison. He switched to another screen and watched as a woman defiantly and angrily verbally pushed back against every question the MSS interrogator put to her. Li checked her "sheet" and found a hard history. She was already on the dangerous list. He didn't want to waste anymore of his time. He sent a message that she was to be tortured until she told everything she knew.

Finally, he got word that the matter he had been waiting for was now underway. He touched the screen with several motions, and was now looking at the questioning of the courier. The man had no ties to dissidents or terrorists, had a perfect and loyal record. By all accounts, he had been a victim of a well-planned attack.

Yet something bothered the minister. In fact, several things troubled him.

Shen came on the line. "Apparently there is no footage from the train," he told his boss.

"Why not?" the minister asked suspiciously.

"A malfunction."

"Too coincidental."

"Of course," Shen said, knowing Li's aversion to coincidences. Some would actually call it an outright fear.

"Any evidence of tampering?"

"Inconclusive at this point, but they're still investigating."

"What are your thoughts?"

"The courier is one of our best and longest-serving. He has an exemplary background. There is nothing tying him to anything or anyone remotely suspicious. He did sustain a gunshot wound to his abdomen, and fired his weapon and attempted to stop the thieves."

"I know all that. Do I need to repeat my question?"

"Are you watching the interrogation?"

"Yes."

"Is he lying?" Shen asked. Li's ability to spot liars was legendary within the MSS.

"I don't know yet."

Shen suspected he did. This wasn't about the courier, it was a test for *him*. "I doubt it was premeditated. It seems impossible that he was involved with the planning, or was somehow compromised. However, there appears to be reason to believe that his story is not complete. That for some reason, he may have cooperated."

"May have given them the code."

"That is my guess."

"Why? Why would he? And why would they leave him alive?"

"I don't know. Could have been a simple deal to spare his life."

"Maybe," Li said, then added almost inaudibly, "Who *are* they?"

"What are you going to do?"

Li answered, at the same time as he sent instructions. "Get everything he knows, then execute him."

Tess, still reeling from the possibility that China had produced living Frankenkids, placed her palm over the biometric sensor. A buzzer sounded and a heavy door opened. She descended a long, wide staircase, the click of her cowboy boots keeping a corner of her mind always in Taos, and entered into what was known as "Bunker W," one of several on the grounds of the CIA Langley, Virginia campus.

The windowless space was sparse, but formal: a polished conference table, surrounded by six plush leather rolling office chairs, a CIA seal on one wall, a framed painting of the Washington, D.C. skyline on the other. The room was equipped with every scrambling and anti-listening tech in existence. Nothing could be overheard in the room, and no electronics, phones, or recording devices would work inside its thick walls.

Two men were waiting for her. The first, an old friend, Dr. J. W. Skyenor, Director of Defense Advanced Research Projects Agency. DARPA, the Pentagon's emerging technology agency, had been formed in 1958 by President Eisenhower after the Soviet Union's surprise success with launching Sputnik, the first man-made object into space, in 1957. One of the agency's earliest accomplishments was helping to launch the world's first weather satellite.

The other, she didn't like at all. Holt Gatewood, administrator of HITE, short for Hidden Information and Technology Exchange, a government entity so classified that most US presidents usually didn't learn about it unless they got a second term. HITE had been established after World War II to handle captured Nazi secrets, technology, and even metaphysical data and artifacts. If a UFO of extraterrestrial origin really did crash in Roswell, New Mexico, during the summer of 1947, HITE would have wound up with the wreckage and whatever it may have contained.

The name was a bit of a misnomer because the hidden technology and/or information was never exchanged. Instead, a select committee made up of top US intelligence leaders—with security clearances *much* higher than the President of the United States—decided who, where, when, and *if* the information would be released. HITE was the ultimate strategic advantage because its members could ignite huge shifts in power and wealth via the introduction of new technologies—be it nuclear weapons, computers, satellites, pharmaceuticals, etcetera.

Tess didn't want to share the information about the Mìng Rénshēng program and specifically Yǐn Huāshù—the hidden flowers. She knew by doing so that Chase and Wen would be put in even more danger, yet there was no choice. She needed Gatewood and Skyenor. With the future of the human race at stake, Chase and Wen might need to be sacrificed for the greater good.

Chapter Twenty-Eight

The tops of the buildings had no rails or walls, just flat, smooth glass to give the full illusion of a waterfall. Somehow, Chase and Wen hit the next building with only thirteen inches to spare. Rolling onto the smooth surface as gunfire shattered the glass around them, Chase came up a split second after Wen, already running across the roof toward the next jump. There were no celebrations for defying gravity and the laws of physics while dodging bullets and running for their lives. Another suicidal leap waited only a second away. This time the enemy knew not just where they were, but where they were going.

"Ready?" Chase yelled as they approached the edge.

"Each one gets easier, right?" Wen yelled back.

Although a little more confident after having survived the first leap, they had less energy, and were flying on nothing but adrenaline and fear. Flinging themselves through space, hoping they would travel as far, they gulped air and avoided looking down. The landing came harder this time, and with only ten inches between them and a deadly plunge. Without stopping, Chase did the math in his head, and realized at that rate, with diminishing returns, by the last jump, they might only have an inch to spare, or conceivably could miss it by three. Even the second to last building could fall short. He kept running as if bullets were still flying past him, even though they weren't, because the MSS teams were moving, already getting into position to intercept them.

"We've got to reach the last building before the agents do!" Wen yelled.

By the next building, their margin was down to five inches. The one after that they only made by two. "We've got to run faster," Chase yelled, panic in his voice. Neither of them had much left, their breaths coming in gasps.

Pounding down onto the three-story building, Chase barely made it. Wen slammed into the side of the slick glass and clung to the roof, kicking against the smooth side, trying to pull herself up before she slipped. Chase had tucked into a roll and gotten to his feet at the same moment he heard her yell. He spun and dove back down on his stomach, grabbing both of Wen's hands, holding her twisting body, reeling against the force of her weight pulling him down. There was nothing to grab on the flat surface.

"I'm losing you!" he yelled as she slid a little more.

"Let me go! I don't want to pull you over with me!"

"No!" he screamed. Rolling onto his side and using strength from an unknown source, he flipped over, using his own body as leverage, and lifted her. She came up on top of him, and they both lay collapsed and spent.

"We're not doing another," she panted.

"No," he agreed.

They stumbled to their feet, ran toward the stairwell hatch, and pulled it open. "They'll know we're in this building," Wen said as they practically poured their bodies down the stairs, their legs on fire, rubbery, almost unable to support themselves. They went down more on the railings than the steps.

"Let's get on the damned elevator!" Chase said.

"Too easy for them to trap us and make it our tomb."

Instead, they continued punishing their legs and knees.

"Where are they now?" Chase gasped.

"Rushing to this building."

"Maybe they saw us go in, but they won't know where if we just pick a floor."

She pointed to a camera in the stairwell as they passed. "They've got handheld portable monitors on them. They'll know. And we have no idea where they are."

"So they could be waiting for us at the bottom."

"We don't even know what this building *is*!"

They continued down the stairs, thankful it was only three stories high, and came out at the bottom into a fitness club. The entire first floor was floor-to-ceiling windows. They could see up the street the line of the waterfall buildings, and the team that was approaching. They knew where Chase and Wen were.

"We have to fight them here," Wen said.

"We might take eight," Chase said, hardly believing his own words, "but if the other sixteen come . . . "

"If the other sixteen come, we'll have more weapons, technology, and monitors."

Chase nodded. If they could defeat these eight and get their gear, they might have a chance, but still, it would be almost impossible.

Chapter Twenty-Nine

Wen quickly surveyed the elaborate three-story fitness center. "That downhill ski slope will be a good spot," she said, pointing up the "mountain," which was complete with a three-chair ski lift.

"And that climbing wall," Chase added, looking over at the other end of the massive space to a realistic rock area that appeared to have several expert levels. An elevated jogging track wove through the rock climbing wall and cliffs all the way back to the ski hill. The track rose on translucent platforms above treadmills, stationary bikes, stair climbers, and, seemingly, all the latest work-out equipment. Glass staircases connected the track.

"We can use the water," Wen said, running across one of the clear bridges. The center of the building featured a pool, with channels going in and out and circling the room. Instead of traditional rowing machines, they had actual sleek rowing crafts. "We can do this," Wen said.

Chase saw many places to hide, and they'd have the

advantage of setting up their positions and waiting. "As long as our ammunition holds out."

"It will if we're ready in time," she said, quickly shooting every camera she could see.

"Okay, you're the warrior, what's the plan?" He knew she'd already been formulating contingencies, looking for weaknesses, advantages, potential attack points, places of concealment, and lines of escape as soon as they'd arrived. Wen laid out her ideas as they moved to higher ground.

A few minutes later, when the first MSS agents came through the entrance with full confidence that their targets were waiting inside, Chase and Wen were ready.

Wen could see, from her vantage point high in the rock cliffs, that the agents were already doing what she knew they would—assessing the space, searching for the same areas of concealment where Chase and Wen would be hiding. She watched as three female agents and five male took the lower room, their eyes on the cliffs, ski hill, and track, because their training (the same as Wen's) told them to get the high ground. However, what they didn't know was they were up against a former top MSS officer, who knew exactly how they would attack the scene.

Wen's confidence grew, knowing they could take out the entire team as long as no additional teams showed up until they were done. She began counting. The timing of her assault needed to be perfect. Chase, on the second level of the track, in a maintenance cubicle not visible from the ground, did not have the skill to shoot from any higher point. Wen also needed him on that level, knowing he would wait for her first move. If the team's response was as she expected, opening in a choreographed series of movements and counter movements imprinted on the agents in their training, she would gain control of the incident rather quickly.

The agents split up into four pairs, each taking a corner. They would funnel up to the higher levels in a search-and-exterminate sequence, culminating in them taking the high ground. Wen continued counting, her scope of vision not as wide as she would've liked, but any other spot would've been too risky. She had gone as high as possible. At that moment she could see all the agents, but soon some would slip into blind spots. Those were the most dangerous, particularly once they got closer to Chase.

Wen counted, measured every step in her mind, worked the angles of bullets, played the scenarios out, sifted, thought . . .

Ten, nine, eight . . .

She tracked two agents as they neared Chase. Two others were taking the ski lift up, two were checking the equipment.

Seven, six . . .

Two agents were near the rock wall, and one of those found the concealed staircase behind the cliff, but Wen had already locked the secure door. The stairs were for maintenance, so staff could get up the cliff without having to climb it.

Five, four . . .

The other two were near the pool. She scanned the vast space with one last sweep to be sure everyone was where she expected them to be.

Three, two, one . . .

Wen shot the two agents on the ski lift. At the same moment, Chase fired as two agents reached his hiding place on the jogging track. One of them was just bending down to look inside, having noticed the space.

Chase stepped over the bodies of the two agents he had just killed. Even knowing they would've killed him an instant later, he still felt remorse. One of them was a woman, and he imagined she might be somebody like Wen—trapped in a system, bred as a killer, oppressed, her every move watched. What if she, like Wen, wanted to escape, had maybe even tried?

The man who had looked in at Chase couldn't have been older than twenty-five. The bullets had ripped open his face, leaving a grotesque, unrecognizable image in Chase's mind.

He used meditative techniques of his Buddhist practice to suppress, for now, the thoughts of the two agents he had just killed. However, some time, a week or two from now, if he were still alive, he'd wake up in the middle of the night, shaking, sweating, seeing their faces, finishing the thoughts that had begun the instant after the bullets had stolen their final breaths, and he would deal with that then, suffer through the repercussions and psychological ramifications of taking a life—or, in this case, two of them, and more to come. All had been in full living mode, trying to survive like everyone else, but now there were more to kill, and he had to do it.

"*Focus,*" he whispered to himself.

Chapter Thirty

Li brought up the feeds from the ghost city.

"What is going on in there?" the MSS minister asked the officer in charge of the operation as he watched footage of sixteen agents approaching the fitness center.

"As you can see, all cameras inside the center have been taken offline. We have limited body cam coverage."

"Yes, I can see that. Our people are dropping fast."

"Targets have an advantage of concealment and preparation."

"We have the advantage of training and numbers. There are two targets. Eight MSS agents ought to be able to apprehend them."

"With all due respect, sir, the targets are not civilians."

"Who are they?" Li asked as two more body-cams went dark.

"I was hoping you knew. However, they have obviously had extensive military training . . . CIA perhaps."

"Not on our soil." Li muted the audio with the officer and opened another line to the head of a specialized division within the MSS, who was working on identifying and reverse tracking the pair that had been causing so much trouble. "I want answers!" Li demanded.

"Minister Li," the man responded, as if addressing the grim reaper. "We are pursuing every angle. Apparently they arrived in Shanghai from Hong Kong."

"They originated in Hong Kong?"

"We don't know yet."

"And Ghost Dragon, Sky Net?" Li asked, referring to the two most important tools for identifying and tracking people that the MSS had.

"Zero definitive results," the man admitted meekly.

Li shook his head. *Now we're tracking actual ghosts. Who are they?*

He ended the connection and reopened the conversation with the Officer in charge of the Ghost City. "Why don't we have them yet?"

"We're going to need additional resources," the officer announced tensely.

"Two people cornered in a vacant fitness center in the middle of an empty city? What should we do?" Li asked, exasperated. "Blow up the building?"

"I think that would be an excellent idea."

Gatewood and Skyenor, in charge of two of the US government's most secretive agencies, which invented or controlled the absolute top technologies on earth, stared at Tess as if she had just told them that time travel were possible.

"They've got *living* specimens?" Gatewood asked incredulously. "For how long."

"Possibly seven years."

Skyenor stared at her. "What are the subjects capable of?"

"We don't know."

"How many IT-Squads are you sending?" Gatewood asked.

"None," she replied.

Gatewood appeared stunned.

"It's China. Deep in country. Dozens of locations—"

"They're altering *human* genes," Gatewood said, as if she didn't know. "This puts the entire human race at stake. I don't give a damn if they're doing it on the moon, we need teams moving on this."

"The president isn't going to risk war with China," Skyenor said, before Tess could.

"We do have people there," she said.

"People?"

"Two."

"*Two?*" Gatewood yelled. "You'd better tell me it's Rambo and Jason Bourne!"

"Something like that. Independents."

His astounded expression silently amused Tess. "Independents? Really? What are they doing?"

"At the moment?" Tess asked. "Getting shot at, I believe."

"Wonderful." Gatewood sounded as if he were about to laugh, but he did not.

"That's why I need your help. It's going to require us to unleash every piece of advanced tech trickery and tech weaponry we possess."

Both men stared at her.

"I mean things we've never used before." She held their gazes. "Things we don't even *have* yet."

The two men understood. There were secrets in Washington, and then there were *deep* secrets, but the real secrets were the ones that *no one* knew. The ones that no one could even imagine, that only existed in the whispers of shadows and the margins of time. These two men and Tess knew most of the deepest secrets the world had to offer. They also knew the invisible ones that were so dangerous they didn't like to think about them too much. These ultimate secrets could only be discussed by the heads of CISS, DARPA, and HITE in a secure bunker underneath the CIA headquarters, and such a conversation had never taken place before. Not even this one. Most especially, not this one.

Chapter Thirty-One

Wen watched Chase run up the jogging track. Its solid surface, some type of rubberized recycled plastic composite material, probably wouldn't stop a bullet, but did provide concealment as it spiraled up toward the top of the space. Those below could not see where he was.

With four other agents still to deal with, Wen had no time to second-guess her plan, but she had hoped to be able to take out the two below her on the rocks. As soon as the gunfire began, they had scattered for cover, and were no longer in her line of sight. Even with that setback, Wen had still been remarkably accurate in her predictions of the agents' reactions. As expected, all four remaining found ways onto the jogging track. She knew her opponents knew that Chase was somewhere on the suspended maze above them, and Wen was somewhere higher.

These agents are trained to pursue the battle even if it means falling into their targets' trap, Wen thought. *We've got to eliminate them before another team arrives.*

The urgency in the realization that each passing second

brought sixteen more agents closer spurred Wen to make an otherwise unnecessarily risky move. She descended down the rock wall among the repelling lines, kicked, and swung out from the wall just far enough to where she could leap onto the jogging trail track. Once on it, she ran toward the enemy. Being one level below Chase, she counted on him seeing her as she crossed an intersection. When their eyes met, she pointed toward the other direction and hoped he understood. Keeping low, so that he would still remain hidden, he ran toward where she'd indicated.

Chase had picked up the guns from the couple he'd killed. Now running toward another shoot-out, he too felt the time pressure. They had to kill the last four and escape somewhere else into the city where they could surprise the remaining teams.

Or, maybe there's some way to escape the city altogether, he thought as he came around one of the long, sweeping curves in the track. He looked over the edge, trying to locate one of them, and instead found himself staring straight into the eyes of an agent looking up at him. They fired at the same time. Chase's high ground advantage and better angle allowed him to survive, yet the bullet grazed his shoulder, leaving him with a stinging pain, ripped shirt, and oozing blood. His victim fell onto a weight machine below.

Another agent unloaded a steady stream of rounds into the upper track where Chase had been, but, anticipating the response, Chase had immediately leapt forward, barely escaping the bullets ripping through the track. The machine gun fire tore a section free, causing part of the track to swing down. Chase kept crawling, desperately fleeing the continuing spray of bullets. He heard more shots across the opening and saw an agent drop from one of the other sections of track, plunging into the pool, transforming the crystal water around her body into a crimson cloud.

Chase scrambled up the track, which rose, then descended again, giving him separation and another angle advantage. He bent around to take a shot, but an MSS agent was waiting, already aiming up in Chase's direction. Just as the man pulled the trigger, Wen shot him from behind. His bullets veered off and missed their mark.

"You okay?" Wen yelled to Chase.

"Yeah, you?"

"No injuries. Let's get out of here before the others show up." Chase looped back around and met her on the track. "Are we sure we don't want to wait here?" Chase asked. "It's a pretty good place to defend, and we've got experience now. They'll eventually find us in the city, probably in a place where they have the advantage."

"You've been spending too much time with me," Wen said, smiling. "You're probably right. Let's get all their weapons." Wen set up the dead agents to look like they were firing down. "From below, they'll only be able to see their arms and the guns," she explained. "They'll draw fire and distract the agents." She caught Chase looking at her arms and hands, covered in fresh blood. "Don't worry, it's not mine. How's your arm?" She rubbed his shoulder, he winced, she inspected it, kissed his sweaty lips, and said, "You should stop playing with guns."

He nodded. No, it wasn't her blood, yet later, when the action was over, she'd be feeling as if it were.

"Keep moving," he told her. "Time is the enemy."

They set up two more agents in other areas, took the rest of the weapons and extra ammo, and quickly discussed the likely attack. Wen found a grenade on the leader. "This will come in handy."

"Just don't use it too close to us." Chase winked.

She winked back at him. "It will only work if they come in together."

Chase discovered a tunnel leading from one section of the pool to another, it was not all underwater, and had a bridge going over it which provided an air pocket. Wen considered setting up in there. They'd never see her, but moving through the water would be slow, and her own visibility would be limited. It was too risky.

She went back on the top of the cliff. This time, Chase ascended the ski hill. Both positions provided them the advantages of having the high ground, and they could not be accessed without the agents exposing themselves. Wen shouted final commands across to Chase. Through the tall glass walls, she could see eight agents coming. As soon as they entered, they began shooting.

Wen tossed the grenade.

Chapter Thirty-Two

The explosion took out five of the eight agents. The remaining three were injured, but still mobile. They immediately began firing upon the "decoy" people. As soon as they went down, the agents, believing they had killed their targets and knowing that there was no one else in the city, lowered their guns and ran up to retrieve the bodies.

Once they were close enough, Chase began shooting and, inconceivably, took out all three agents. He didn't like guns, but couldn't deny their effectiveness. He was about to make the same mistake the agents did and run out into the open, but Wen yelled, "More!"

He could see out the glass walls that eight fresh agents were about to pour into the fitness club.

Wen skied down the "mountain," machine guns blazing, and killed three before veering off, jumping a row of bikes, pulling off the skis, and while still in midair, managed to get one boot off before landing in the pool. She hit the water awkwardly, going in sideways. Chase ran across the jogging track he now knew so well, but before he could reach her, two agents sprayed a hail of bullets toward him. The track blew apart as the machine gun fire followed him. Fragments of two bullets tore into his calf, and Chase went down.

Wen wrestled with the other ski boot underwater. Freeing herself, she surfaced and did an instant three-hundred-sixty-degree survey of the fitness center. Unable to see Chase, she swam for the closest side, but had to go back under to avoid incoming fire. She swam to the bridge and came up in the air pocket.

Chase stayed down, waiting, and clutching his leg.

Wen waited, too. While the agents fired repeatedly into the pool, she slipped out on the other side of the bridge, found a dead agent, and traded guns. She quickly slipped her shoes from her pack, put them back on, and loaded up with additional magazines from the wasted agent. He was the leader of the squad because he also had four grenades and a combat knife. She took them all and crawled through the bodies and wreckage of earlier attacks. Noticing one agent was badly injured but still breathing, Wen quickly broke his neck to end the suffering.

Unable to use a grenade so close to Chase, she got within ten feet of three of the agents before they spotted her, but by then it was too late. With them dead, there were only two remaining, and she didn't know where they were.

She climbed up a fallen section of the track and slithered over to Chase. "You're hit?"

"It doesn't seem too bad."

"Can you get down?"

"Yeah. Can we leave yet? I'm tired of all the exercise."

Wen spotted where the last two were. "Oh no," she said. "Look out the window. Those two are regrouping with a fresh team of eight!"

He saw them running toward the fitness center. "Where are they coming from? I thought we finished—"

Wen helped him down and grabbed a first aid kit hanging on the wall. "We're leaving," she said.

"But this place has been good to us. We've had three victories, we just need to do it one more time."

"No, we need to go." Wen had long believed the law of averages, diminishing returns, and of some blurred fringe of karma. She didn't think they would find success a fourth time at the fitness center. "They'll just keep coming."

"But—"

"It's like jumping from the buildings. Each time we got a couple inches closer to the edge, until we weren't going to make one more jump." She had never stopped pushing them toward the back door. They burst out into a parking area and quickly crossed the street to the next building in the waterfall series. It gleamed silver and blue, and although it was a stationary building with no moving effects, in the sunlight against the reflecting blue sky, the building looked like running water, as if it were part of a cascading falls. The architect had been a master.

In spite of the intense pain in Chase's calf, they kept running until they passed the final single story building, which seemed more like a reflecting pool topped with mist.

"Where are we going?" Chase asked breathlessly.

"When we were jumping off the buildings, I saw a parking lot with cars."

"You did?" Chase marveled that she could somehow sightsee while remaining focused on the deadly jump.

"I'm not sure. It was just in my peripheral vision, but I believe another few blocks this way, and maybe one or two over to the north."

Chase figured they didn't have much of a lead on the

ten agents, who would have already entered the fitness center and discovered twenty-two dead bodies, but no Chase or Wen. They would have checked the cameras and would know exactly where they were.

Wen was coming to those conclusions in a different way, counting, timing, calculating, visualizing the MSS's every move. In her mind, she saw the agents as if in a movie. She anticipated they would count the missing weapons and quickly assess the risk and possible scenarios—and they would know everything. She could see them checking tablets and pulling up the surveillance feeds.

Wen had to make do with the movie in her head, estimating how long each element would take them, and knowing that by now additional support would be arriving in the ghost city. Helicopters would soon descend. She calculated how long it would take them to get in the air, distance they would be traveling and speed. "Helicopter gunships will be in the city in less than twenty minutes, probably two of them, and two more carrying another twenty-four agents each."

"We can't outrun a gunship. I don't care what kind of car we get."

Chapter Thirty-Three

Wen estimated that they had a four minute, twelve seconds lead, but that advantage could evaporate at any moment. The real reason they were still alive was the MSS didn't yet know Wen's identity. They didn't understand that she knew all their tactics, and could use that knowledge to defeat them. Had they known that one of their targets was an invisible MSS agent just like them—better than them, one of the best ever—they would have waited for more teams and altered their attack.

Wen also credited their survival to the fact that she and Chase had the wild power of freedom. Instead of serving the oppressors, the evil masters, they served the better good and had righteousness on their side. She believed that had power to it. Maybe not a power worth forty-eight more agents on top of the final ten still after them, and certainly not equal to a helicopter gunship, but worth quite a bit, nonetheless.

They ran as if the hounds of hell were nipping at their

heels. Chase was sure he had never moved so fast, and didn't know where the oxygen was coming from, powering his lungs to push the blood into his legs to take the pounding on his bleeding calves. Wen, still wet from the pool, changed her equations with each step, recalibrating the timing every second. Three minutes and fifty-two seconds, three minutes-forty—her mind continued the process while they moved. Another part of her brain scanned ahead, looked at every scenario and every potential threat. It was easier than usual, since they were in an empty city.

"It's just crazy how dystopian it feels," Chase said breathlessly as they ran down another block, devoid of people and vehicles, but otherwise a normal modern metropolis. "I can't help but feel that we're somehow the last survivors in a post-apocalyptic world. Like a plague or some mysterious thing wiped out humanity and it's just us."

"I think that would be quite wonderful. Not the wiping out of humanity part, but just us, alone," Wen said, still counting as they continued searching for the elusive parking lot.

"Look." Chase pointed across to a bus terminal with at least three dozen buses lined up. Wen, estimating the agents were now only two minutes and forty-eight seconds behind them, rapidly considered all the potential scenarios of trying to take a bus instead of a smaller vehicle. "Should we?" Chase asked.

"We could still be two blocks or more away from the cars," Wen admitted. "They could be on us before we get there. I don't think we have a choice. Let's do it."

The buses were in a narrow space between two skyscrapers, a multi-story atrium and skybridge connecting the two buildings. The buses were parked underneath, and more seemed to be in an underground parking area.

They boarded a sleek city bus and Chase went to work. Wen kept watch, her submachine gun ready, and counted, estimating how long it would take to get it started.

"Our margin is dwindling," she announced. "We've got two minutes."

"Doesn't matter. Our luck has turned," Chase said. "The keys are here." The bus roared to life, and a second later it rumbled out of the depot with Chase behind the wheel and Wen running freely through the empty passenger section with the bag of machine guns and grenades she'd confiscated from the fallen MSS agents.

The pursuers were on foot, while Chase and Wen rode in a "tank." Preparing for battle, she smashed out the back windows and several side ones.

"Where are we going?" Chase yelled back.

"Airport!" Wen shouted.

"There's an airport?"

"This is a city built for millions of people, of course there is. A rather nice one, I would imagine."

"Where is it?"

Wen was already pulling up the area on her phone while keeping an eye out the back window. "We're not going to get far in this bus once the gunship shows up." Their new sense of liberation would instantly vanish as soon as a small missile demolished the bus. "Our only hope is the airport."

"If we can reach it in time."

"It's the next street," She told him looking at the local mapping she'd downloaded from the security office. "Turn right."

"Okay, I see it." He cranked the big wheel, made the

turn, half expecting to see a blockade of tanks or military vehicles, but there was nothing, just like everywhere else—an empty, urban wasteland, other than the fact that his imagined post-apocalyptic version was full of battered zombies and burnt-out vehicles. This one he found himself in was shiny and new, but there were still "monsters" after them.

"What are we going to do once we're at the airport? You don't really think there's going to be any departures, do you?"

"I'll know once we get there."

The sound of machine gun fire ended their conversation. It had come from a side street they'd just passed. Four agents sped their way in a police car, two of them leaning out windows, firing. Chase checked the rearview mirror as a pickup truck with the other six came screaming up behind.

Wen was already in full retaliation, alternating between the back window and the side.

"I'm not hitting anything, but it's keeping them at a safe distance," she yelled, frustrated by the swerves, speed, and bumps preventing her from taking any decent shots. Within half a block, the cat and mouse game grew uglier as the pursuers pressed for an advantage and became more brazen. The pickup truck driver was particularly daring, coming up fast and hard. Chase was convinced the man was planning to ram the back of the bus, but the driver's mistake, like the others who now lay dead back at the fitness center, was that he underestimated Wen. Of course, he couldn't have known her training, but when the pickup truck exploded, killing everyone on board, the driver's last thought might have been, *"Who the hell is this woman?"*

Wen considered herself lucky. The agents had been

sloppy, a little too desperate to capture the people that had killed so many agents and done who knows what else. They should've known that grenades were missing and not gotten so close to the bus.

Four more in the police car, she thought. *And then the gunship.*

Chapter Thirty-Four

Wen tried to get a clean shot at the police car at the same time as Chase used the bus's size to force them off the road. Unfortunately, in the frantic race, their attempts to stop the MSS agents were at odds with each other. As soon as Wen had a shot lined up, Chase's driving would throw her off when he smashed into the car again. Glass shattered as the last of the windows were blown out by machine gun fire. Wen gave up trying to go for the tires as she was jostled and bounced around in the back of the bus. She tossed another grenade, but the police car was harder to hit as it charged and retreated parallel to them, and it missed the target. Meanwhile, Chase saw on the dashboard GPS map that he had an upcoming right-hand turn, which might give him the opportunity to sandwich the police car.

"I'm going to be making a sharp right up ahead!" Chase yelled back.

"To the airport?" Wen replied.

"Yeah, it'd be great if we could shake them before we catch our flight."

"Be great if we could shake them at all," Wen said. *Maybe I can feed them a grenade.* She checked the angles while running to the middle of the bus. Several incoming bursts of gunfire tore through the metal frames where the windows used to be. She dove to the floor. "No signals, I need to surprise them."

It amused Chase that Wen thought he might actually put the blinker on and obey traffic laws while he was in an empty city, in the middle of China, being chased by a carload of killers. "You got it," he yelled back.

Wen got to her feet, double checked, and decided she could make the toss. Watching the police car, knowing her two advantages—the bus's size and the fact that the agents had no idea they were about to turn—might be enough.

Above the noise of the revving motor, squealing tires, and intermittent burst of machine gun fire, Wen's highly trained ears listened for the one thing that would not only doom her plan, but could prevent them from escaping the ghost city. Luckily, at least for now, she heard no approaching helicopter. Still, she knew MSS protocol too well . . .

The silence in the air won't last much longer. They're coming, she thought. *They're almost here.*

"Ready?" Chase yelled back.

"Yes." Wen had already been counting down. The turn was eight seconds away. Careful to stay out of sight, she braced herself between two seats in the front section and counted. *Seven seconds.* Another round of machine gun fire pierced the side of the bus, stray bullets puncturing the roof above her. She suddenly worried they might know her location inside the bus.

Five seconds . . .

Chase didn't even slow down. Although, he'd never

driven a bus before, and wasn't sure if it could make the tight, ninety degree turn doing sixty mph, without flipping, he didn't want them to have any clue the turn was coming.

Four seconds . . . three . . .

Wen pushed the detonation button on the grenade, a new, advanced model that the MSS had developed especially for their agents. It would go off in four seconds.

At the last moment, Chase applied just enough pressure to the brakes, hoping he wasn't about to roll the bus into the intersection and destroy their only chance of escape.

Two seconds . . . One . . .

Wen stood and tossed the grenade out the window toward the police car without even taking time to look. The car either had to be there, or not. In that same instant, Chase ripped the steering wheel around.

Wen, holding tightly on to the seat and the window frame, steadied herself as wheels lifted off the road, the bus tilted, and the grenade landed on the hood of the police car. She fought to hold on and stay on her feet for a horrible, wobbly moment, thinking the bus was going to go over.

The grenade exploded on the police car, shattering the windshield, just as the bus came back down onto the street, sliding to complete the turn. Chase stomped the accelerator again, the huge vehicle surging to resume its rolling thunder. As they came around the corner, Chase silently thanked the urban gods that there were no pedestrians or other vehicles that could cross his path.

"They're still coming," Wen shouted, chiding herself for not throwing the grenade four-tenths of a second later. It was difficult to tell, but it appeared that at least one of them was dead, the driver possibly seriously injured. "I've got two grenades left. We might have to try a side shot."

"Do it."

"Problem is, with their erratic pursuit and your crazy driving, I can't be sure of a hit."

"Shoot them!"

"Same issues."

"Do you want to drive?"

"Ram them!" she yelled. "Keep ramming them."

"As fun as it is slamming a twenty-ton bus into that little police car filled with men trying to kill us, isn't as easy as it looks." Chase swerved, but the police car went up on the sidewalk and avoided the hit. "This thing maneuvers like a U-Haul going through jello." He looked in a side view mirror, spun the giant steering wheel, and went in for another crunch. This one was quite effective, as he managed to send the police car into the side of a building. Somehow the resulting crash caused giant smoke-colored windows to shatter and rain shards of glass in and around the police car.

Wen seized the opportunity to unload a full magazine into the car. Apparently the driver had been injured badly by the grenade blast, because for the first time, they had allowed themselves to be pinned. Wen didn't waste time putting in a new magazine, she just grabbed another gun and poured more rounds into the car as Chase pulled away.

"Do you think we got him?" Chase yelled back as he floored it in the direction of the airport.

"No survivors," Wen yelled back as the police car veered off the sidewalk, zoomed across the road, and crashed into a shoe store.

Chase was happy to be able to drive to the airport, hoping for clear sailing now, but he knew it was hard on Wen whenever she had to kill people—particularly MSS agents, since she saw herself in every single one of them.

Wen gathered their weapons, held onto the two

remaining grenades, and came up to sit in the seat behind Chase. She put her hand on his shoulder. He checked the GPS display in the dash.

"Just two more miles to the airport," he said. "Are you okay?" He didn't just mean had she been injured, he meant was she bleeding emotionally.

Wen answered by shushing him, and he knew she was listening for helicopters.

"Do you hear one?"

She shushed him again. "The gunship is here."

Chapter Thirty-Five

The helicopters and gunship grew closer. Chase held the accelerator to the floor as they entered the airport, the bus crashing through a series of chain-link fences.

"Why would there be planes here?" Chase asked after seeing several smaller planes parked along the side of the runway. "There's nobody here to fly them. This place is ridiculous."

"The city is probably slated to be populated in the next few months. Other ghost cities might have the buildings, but nothing else yet. They do it in stages." She pointed toward several private hangers. "Go there."

Chase steered the battered bus toward a large white building.

"Try that one."

"So in sixty days or whatever, a million people are just going to show up with moving vans?"

"Something like that." Wen estimated the chopper might be in shooting range now.

"Pretty incredible when a country with this many people

and this much money is run by a handful of communist men." He steered the big vehicle up to the entrance of the hangar Wen had indicated.

"Drive into it!"

"I don't see where?"

"Aim for the door, hit the gas—it'll open!"

The "passenger tank" punched through the side of the hanger as if it were a fist through a wet paper bag.

Wen grabbed her duffel of guns and they both exited the bus. Five corporate jets were parked inside. Wen jogged to the one closest to the bay doors and paused. "There's four helicopters," she said, looking up through the high windows. She boarded the plane. "Get the bay doors open!"

Chase didn't have time to question her. *How are we going to fly a plane?* he wondered, actually worried, as he unlatched the big doors and found a button that would slide them back. The jet's engines suddenly drowned out the noise from the approaching helicopters. When he turned and started running to the plane, he saw it was already rolling toward him. As it picked up speed, heading for the opening, Chase jogged next to it, and timed a jump into the open door. Inside, he quickly closed the door.

"Nice plane," he said, joining Wen in the cockpit.

"Glad you like it. Buckle up."

"You can fly jets?"

"Sure," Wen said casually. "I mean, a 747 might be a little tricky, but I could handle it."

"But you've flown one of these?" Chase asked, surprised he was just learning this about her.

"Taking off and flying, no problem, I've just never landed before," she said as they got airborne.

"*What?* Don't you think that could be a problem?" he

asked, sitting in the copilot's seat but not doing anything to assist. "I mean, eventually we'll run out of fuel."

"Oh, I've done it in a simulator a few times."

"Are you kidding?"

She laughed. "Yes."

"Where do you plan to land?" Chase asked, a little more relieved that she could actually land.

"I have no idea."

Chase groaned.

"My main objective was to get out of the ghost city before more MSS helicopters showed up, but now we have a new goal."

"What's that?"

"Getting safely to the ground before Chinese PLA fighter jets shoot us out of the sky."

"They would do that?" he asked, already knowing the answer.

"I'm certain they've already been scrambled."

"How soon will they be here?"

"Twelve minutes."

"*Twelve minutes!?*"

"Or less."

"Here comes the gunship," Chase yelled, pointing.

Wen increased speed and pushed the jet down the empty runway as one of the Chinese helicopters zoomed at them.

"Damn!" Wen shouted. "It's a Z-10."

"What's that?"

"Attack helicopter, advanced tech, anti-tank, air-to-air. Looks like this one is equipped with 30-mm cannons, and TY-90 missiles. May even have unguided rocket pods."

Chase grimaced as the menacing black chopper flew

directly toward them, as if challenging them to an evil game of chicken. "He's blocking our path."

"Yeah, but he hasn't fired yet."

"*Yet* being the key word!" Chase yelled as the jet picked up speed.

"No, *hasn't* is the key word. He should have already blown us to pieces."

"Why hasn't he?"

"Our friends think they can intimidate us. That we won't take off."

"Our friends might be right."

"Not today." As the jet reached top speed, Wen pushed the throttle to the max.

"We're going to fly right into them!" Chase yelled.

"They'll move."

"Why?"

"Because they have orders to take us into custody, not to kill us."

"How do you know?"

"Because we're still alive."

Chapter Thirty-Six

The Z-10 attack helicopter flew unwaveringly at them, leaving them no room to complete their takeoff.

"Hold on!" Wen snapped. "We're going for a rocket climb!"

Before Chase could start to imagine what that even was, Wen pulled the stick and the plane left the ground at an impossible angle, throwing Chase back against his seat as the g-forces fought every normal law of physics his body was used to experiencing.

The Z-10 dropped below them. As Chase recovered from the takeoff that was more like a lift off, he braced for the incoming missile.

"I don't lose at chicken," Wen said, a touch of amusement in her voice.

"They aren't shooting," Chase said.

Wen brought the jet level. "They don't have to. They can follow us and track us on radar. The PLA fighter jets can take us out at will."

"Do you have any great ideas about how to avoid PLA fighter jets?"

"Yeah, I think we can use your multitool."

"Really?"

She laughed wickedly, releasing stress more than anything. "You almost bought into it."

Chase forced a laugh. "Seriously, what's the plan?"

"Our only chance is to be on the ground before the jets get here."

"How much time do you think we have?"

"That is harder to gauge, since the PLA is a different command-and-control than the MSS, but not long. I would guess minutes—under ten."

Chase looked out the window, hunting for a place they could land, not wanting to hit the ground in a shower of debris.

"We have to find somewhere that can handle this plane," Wen said.

"What about heading back to the ghost city? Great runways there. Like new. Hardly been used. Available for the low, low price of free."

"Are you forgetting about the helicopters?"

"Don't you think they're gone by now?"

"No, I think they landed and are cleaning up the mess we made."

"Oh yeah, forgot about that. I'm going to the back to see if there's anything we can use." Chase unbuckled himself and entered the main cabin. There was nothing there except for out-of-the-showroom fresh leather chairs and mahogany-finished tables. Then he saw something that might be useful.

"They just radioed me," Wen said over the pilot's intercom. "Someone official, no doubt following MSS orders.

Told me to turn around and land back at our originating airport or we'll be shot down."

Chase raced back to the cockpit. "What did you reply?"

"I wasn't planning on answering them," Wen said. "I don't like either of their choices."

For whatever reason, he just loved her even more. "Yeah, either way, we die. Maybe if we land somewhere else there's still a chance."

"If we land, the chances are the same. We either wind up in a Chinese prison for a long, long time, and will be dead anyway, or they kill us immediately, as if we never existed."

"Once again, neither of those sounds very attractive."

"I still don't think they're going to shoot us down." She looked over at Chase, as if to say, *But I'm not sure, we could be dead any second.* "They could have done that with the Z-10."

"I don't see them letting us just fly off to Hong Kong."

"There's not enough fuel to make it Hong Kong, but they know that, too. We can't fly forever."

"Why didn't they shoot us down back there?"

"They want to keep us alive," Wen said, still searching for landing sites.

"Because they want to know who we are," Chase guessed. "And they want to know what we're after."

"Yes, and what we did with the information from the courier. Look what they've already sent after us. The Míng Rénshēng program has to be their highest priority national security issue. If we die, they don't know where the trail goes, or who else is out there."

Chase nodded. "Then we can use that."

"Only as long as the fuel holds out, because as soon as we land, they'll be waiting."

"Unless we don't land," Chase said.

She looked at him.

"You're no good at landings anyway."

"I never said that."

"Does this thing have autopilot?" Chase asked.

Wen gave him an inquisitive glance. "Of course."

"What if we jump?"

"Jump?"

"There are parachutes back there."

Her eyes widened. "That might work. I can get to a low cruising altitude. They'll think we're trying to avoid radar. Set the autopilot . . . "

"Then we jump."

"If we get out before the jets get here, they'll just keep following the empty plane."

Chase nodded. "Can you set a course for some distant city so our flight plan looks real?"

"Yes, but . . . have you ever jumped out of a plane?"

"No, but I've always wanted to. Have you?"

She nodded, but gave him a look as if to say, *Of course I have, I was a top MSS operative. We trained on everything short of moon landings.*

"Great, then it's a plan."

"Wait a minute," she said. "I'm not sure you realize how *hard* jumping out of a plane is."

"Come on, we've got to do it quick. If the jets show up, it won't work. You said yourself we're dead either way, and sweetheart, do I have a choice?"

"Okay. You're right. When it comes to dying, it's always better to choose the method of death."

Chapter Thirty-Seven

Tess, Gatewood, and Skyenor adjourned their unprecedented meeting underneath CIA headquarters with a decision that only three individuals should never be allowed to make without congressional oversight, presidential approval, and substantial input from many more experts. However, they had come to an agreement, one that could lead to World War III, and, at the very least, would likely mean Chase and Wen would never leave China alive.

Wen set the autopilot for a faraway city at the end of their fuel range, then ran back to assist Chase in getting his chute on. "Are you *sure* you want to do this?" she asked as she tightened one of the straps.

"No I don't. Got any better ideas?"

"No good ones."

"Where are we going to land?"

"Don't think about that. We'll deal with that once we're

down. Remember, pull this cord as soon as you see me pull mine."

"What if I don't see you pull yours?"

"Pull it when you're about two-thirds down. Make sure you have at least two thousand feet."

Chase looked at her nervously.

"Don't worry, I won't let you die." She opened the door. "I took it as low as I could. Hopefully they'll believe the avoiding radar idea."

The noise from the wind and jet's engine were so loud, Chase barely heard her.

"Ready?"

He gave her a thumbs up. Wen guided him to the edge. Chase felt as if he were going to be sucked out of the plane. He clung to the side of the door frame.

"Go!" She shoved him out, then leaned out, pushed the button to close the door again, and jumped after him. She saw him dropping straight down and positioned her body to soar toward him.

Chase tried to look back up at the plane, but couldn't get his body to cooperate. Instead, he flipped, and was facing down, watching the earth flying up at him. Panic overtook, and he suddenly felt disorientated. Climbing skyscrapers in a window washer rig didn't come close to preparing him for the sheer force of this plummet. He frantically tried to find Wen as he spun through the air. Chaos filled his mind.

What the hell is one-third, or two-thirds down? What does thirds toward the ground even mean? Chase tried to clear his mind. He attempted to swim through the sky, looking for her. *Maybe I should pull the cord now, but maybe I'm still too high.* He flipped again. *Where is she?* Chase tried to overcome the panic by using Buddhism meditation practices. *Deep breaths. Breathe. Breathe. Breathe.*

He finally managed to look up and was amazed to see the plane flying away by itself, but still couldn't see Wen anywhere. *Is the plane really flying on auto pilot? Or, is Wen still on board for some reason?* He tried to wave at the plane, but all it did was send him into a wild somersault.

The wind pummeled his face, as if he were in a fist fight with the sky. His injured leg burned. It hurt so much he tried to see if it was on fire. *I was going to die today anyway. Even if I don't survive this jump, this is a better way to go. Breathe. Breathe.* He looked around, still trying to find her, confused, worried she had vanished. Chase choked on the realization that in the endlessly open sky, Wen didn't seem to be anywhere.

Chase reached his hand up, keeping it near the cord, yet not wanting to touch it, afraid he would pull it too soon. His breathing more controlled now, he looked below again and could only see forests.

What if I land alone, without her? How long will it take for the MSS to pick me up? What kind of wilderness am I going to have to survive in? Why haven't I learned Mandarin yet? Where is she? What happened to her? Breathe. Breathe.

He looked up again, saw their plane, surprisingly far away, flying steady and straight, and was relieved there were still no PLA jet fighters in sight.

The trees were coming up faster now. *I've got to pull the cord*, but his hand was numb, and he didn't know which side

. . .

Chapter Thirty-Eight

Suddenly Wen sailed in next to him, as if powered by jet packs. His sense of relief and joy at seeing her caused him to shout her name three times, but she couldn't hear him, and it made him dizzy to gulp so much air. Wen grabbed his arm. His giant smile told her he was happy to see her. She was also smiling, a reassuring smile, knowing how frightening a first-time jump is, solo and desperate. Wen squeezed his arm. They were together.

She pointed down, and then, with the hand that wasn't holding his, opened and closed it four times, and made a pulling motion, indicating twenty seconds until they would pull the cord. To Chase, twenty seconds seemed like an eternity, certain in ten seconds they would smash into the ground, and surely by twenty they'd be a thousand feet into the earth. It took all his willpower to stop himself from immediately pulling the cord, but he trusted her completely. He didn't know how many planes she had jumped out of, but knew it had probably been a lot, and was not about to question her training or her counting abilities.

They were still holding hands and Chase planned to never let go. He tried not to look down as the ground seemed to be sucking them in like a giant magnet. He strained to look above to find their plane again. It should still be in sight, but he couldn't find it.

Wen tapped him, squeezed his hand, and made the symbol for three seconds. *Where did those last seventeen go?* he wondered. It felt as if he had swallowed the seconds, like he'd swallowed everything—the terror of loss, the confusion, the approaching ground, the pursuing MSS . . .

He struggled to look up again; still no sign of jet fighters. He marveled how Wen could control her body so effortlessly. He'd ask her when they were on the ground if she'd seen their plane, if they'd cleared it before the jet fighters showed up—or the ground.

The ground . . .

He looked down again. Wen squeezed his hand and they both pulled their cords. Her hand was ripped from his as the chutes deployed The sudden deceleration stunned him for a moment. Then all he could think was, "What a Rush!" The jolt and sensation of no longer falling at terminal velocity left him dizzy, as if the air had been stolen from his lungs, a whole new sense of disorientation, but at least now he was floating. Somehow, he got his head up enough so that he could see the full open chute above him.

It's bigger than I thought. Big, beautiful, and billowing full of air, precious air, that air will take me to the ground . . . safely floating.

Chase worried that the approaching fighters would be able to see that big beautiful chute from miles away. *The satellites can probably see it. What are the capabilities of the Chinese? Will our plan even work? Ultimately, it doesn't matter if the MSS believes we're still in the plane.* He continued to fall, this time gentle and controlled. *We just need to get safely to the ground, to touch that incredible firm earth, then we'll figure it out.* He looked down and saw nothing but trees, imagined getting hung up in the top of a hundred and fifty foot pine, unable to get down. *I'm not like this. I don't scare this easily. What's wrong? But jumping out of a plane at four thousand feet, to the mind, is a kind of suicide, to the emotions.* Chase knew he would never be the same again. He had taken another, somewhat unwilling, step toward fearlessness. Jumping off buildings and now an airplane, all in one day.

Where is she? He struggled to search and couldn't believe he'd lost track of Wen a second time. Then, not more than two hundred feet away, above him and off to the right, he saw her chute, her beautiful chute, beautiful Wen. She smiled.

They were going to make it safely to the ground, they were going to be together, alive. The ground. The closer it got, the faster it came. He wondered if they were falling too fast, looked back to Wen, and was happy to see no panic in her face. A few seconds later, they were just above the trees. Wen steered her chute and yelled to Chase to do the same. He could hear her now, and began mimicking her, impressed he had some control. Remarkably, his feet touched the tops of the pine trees, as if he was running on top of them, and then, miraculously, there was a clearing, smaller than two tennis courts, but enough.

Wen went down into the center of it as if hitting a target. Chase came down hard. His injured leg screamed its displeasure at the abuse. He quickly pulled them up and lost what control of the landing he would have had. The wind caught his slowly collapsing chute, pulling him sideways into one of the trees. Pine needles, sap, and breaking branches ripped into him, but he was there. He lived, only slightly more injured than he already was, but in the middle of a tangled mess of branches, paracord, and nylon fabric. By the time he got himself righted, Wen was there. Her chute was already folded into a ball, and she began trying to get his chute untangled. Chase helped and they got most of it. She used a knife to cut away the rest, then took the whole mess and hid it under broken branches.

Chase moved toward her as fast as his injured and wobbly legs would allow. "Wow, I don't think I ever want to do that again."

"Let's hope we don't have to," she replied.

They stared into each others eyes, with a kind of look that people who, together, survived a near death experience would share—one of bundled terror, relief, gratitude, and the knowledge they still had each other.

Chapter Thirty-Nine

Minister Li added several names to his list of those who were going to be punished for allowing the fugitives to escape the ghost city in a corporate jet.

Shen had returned to Li's office upon learning of the greatest loss of MSS agents inside China on a single day, and tried to temper the minister's wrath.

"They won't be able to get away now." Shen pointed to a screen showing the plane, trailed by two fighters. "We're projecting every possible landing site, and we'll be ready."

"Who are these people?"

"CIA? Mossad? I'm not sure anybody else could pull this off." Shen wanted to voice again their earlier conversation about talking to the president, but he knew now wasn't the time. The priority now was to identify and stop the fugitives before more damage was done. "Their evasive tactics against six MSS teams makes it clear that these are not terrorist or dissidents, but the unthinkable . . . enemy agents."

The two men watched the planes on a large monitor.

"Has the president been informed?"

"Yes. He wanted the plane shot down."

Shen was surprised that the plane was still flying.

"I explained that we have to know who is on that plane, and who they are working for."

Shen nodded, impressed. "Anything new on where they are headed?" He pulled up the computer generated report showing their course.

"I don't think they know. They're just trying to escape our agents."

"On their current course, this is the last place they could land." Shen pointed to a city on the screen.

"I don't believe they'll go that far. They're too smart. They'll put it down in the first place with a good landing field."

"Of course that would be their best chance of survival, but they haven't deviated from this flight path since the fighters joined them."

"Because they want us to think they're going there."

"I assume they still haven't responded to any radio request?"

"They are maintaining absolute radio silence. Ignoring us."

"Because they know we won't shoot them down."

Li nodded gravely.

Shen made a call and ordered someone to triple-check every potential airfield, landing strip, highway, or parking lot where they could land.

"Based on what happened in the city," Li said, once Shen was off the phone, "they might just be able to get away again, particularly since we won't be able to put a sizable force in every single one of those potential locations."

"Then perhaps the president is right," Shen said.

"If they land where we don't have a response, the fighters will blow their plane."

"There is a possibility that they didn't have time to share the data they took from the courier."

"I've considered that," Li said.

"But you want to know for sure?" Shen asked.

"I want to question them personally, and once I'm satisfied with the answers, I want to personally pull the trigger and watch them die," the minister replied.

Shen looked surprised.

"You believe I'm an important man in China," Li said, looking suddenly older, "and if I was, what power I had was diminished today when we lost twenty-four agents and the courier's security . . . that is under our jurisdiction. It is my failing."

"But your recommendation—"

"My recommendations do not matter, whether they were followed or not, because we failed to protect the labs' data, and we failed, even more miserably, in apprehending the suspects."

"What if we fail again?" Shen asked, being the only person who could question the minister and challenge Li's decision. "What happens if we don't shoot that plane down and these fugitives, these foreign agents, whoever they are, get away? Even if they never do another thing, the fact that they've gotten away would be a tremendous crime. Do we really want to risk that?"

The minister knew the question actually was did *he* want to risk it. "I have to take that chance. If we kill them now, in the air, they take all their secrets with them." He looked back at the plane. "We have to know," he said quietly, visibly fatigued.

Shen nodded. "We have tightened security at all the facilities, implemented your original recommendations, and we're hunting every possible accomplice. Images of the fugitives from the city and the train have been circulated nationwide and to our agents internationally. If they are known, we will surely learn something soon."

Chapter Forty

Wen pulled out a compass. "There's a village not too far, this way," she said.

"How do you know?"

"I saw it while we were falling."

"Amazing," Chase said. "I couldn't even figure out which way was up most of the time."

"Listen," she said. A second later, Chase heard the distinct sound of approaching jet fighters. "I think we got away with it."

"They might have been close enough to have seen us," Chase said.

Through a break in the trees, they watched as the fighters closed in on their plane—now, a small dot in the distance—at supersonic speed. Soon a fighter was flying above each wing of their plane, then all three vanished from view.

Wen whistled. "They think we're still on the plane!"

"We did it!" Chase yelled.

"As long as helicopters don't show up in the next ten minutes or so, I think we did."

"Let's hope this village of yours has a car we can borrow."

"And that they have cell coverage," she said, checking a phone.

"Yeah, that too," Chase said, as they trudged through the forest. They needed to get in touch with WOLF, the Astronaut, and Tess. "Hopefully, Tess has been able to come up with something for us."

They discussed what they did know, the information from the courier, and the fact that they were going to have to go inside one of the labs to get the proof they needed.

"Everything will be harder now," Wen said. "The MSS will be all over this, and we're inside China." She made a pained expression.

"Their playground, their rules," Chase said, trying to hide a limp.

"I'm afraid they're going to put heavy pressure on WOLF." Wen, who never missed a detail, stopped and bent down to check his wound.

"Aaah!"

"Your injury doesn't look good . . . can you make it to the village, or should I jog ahead?"

"If I don't have to run."

They moved on.

"China has more than one and a half billion people," Wen continued. "The state goes to great lengths to control them, to make sure no one challenges the party's authority. With that many people, they know there are many dissidents, and it is a constant battle for them to find them all, yet at the same time, in some cases, they look the other way." She stopped to check the compass. "They don't want to crack down too hard in order to create more dissidents, but for this, they will look for everyone. They will go after the people they suspect, with or without proof. Hundreds, probably thousands, will be jailed in the next few days. And they'll turn the screws to come up with our names and what we have."

"We're running out of time. We need to leave China tonight."

"What if Tess comes up with information on Yĭn Huāshù?" Wen asked.

Chase had not forgotten about the rumored lost children, the hidden flowers. "We have to find them."

"Then we need more time."

Li looked at the images of Chase and Wen. Although their identities were altered by the vIDs, the virtual Image Deviation system had limitations—it could not change the sex or race of a subject.

"A westerner and a Chinese woman . . . it does not bode well."

Li thought back on another recent case where he had also been pursuing a westerner and a Chinese woman, and pulled up his files while Shen monitored MSS operations.

Agents were raiding more suspected dissidents and arrest totals were already in the hundreds. One of the larger screens showed eight MSS agents storming a house on the outskirts of a small city. They'd been given orders to use all attempts to avoid killing suspects—needed for interrogation —unless escape appeared imminent. In those situations, lethal force was authorized. Shen watched the bouncy chest-cam as two men ran out the back of the shabby house, one of them armed. The MSS agents pursued through yards, up a residential street, down an alley, between a small animal corral, until they were cornered and the men engaged with the MSS. With superior training and firepower, the agents quickly killed both men.

Shen immediately made a call. He wanted the group of remaining people, who had been successfully apprehended at the house, to be red flagged. "I want to be involved in the interrogation." He told his subordinate to arrange a remote video feed. It was unusual that somebody would be armed, even more unusual that they would attempt to fight their way out. "They were protecting something, or someone." He watched other screens as similar events occurred in different cities, in apartment buildings, small shops, private businesses, a warehouse in Hong Kong. The two men from that house had been the only fatalities, which reinforced his hunch and their importance.

However, it would take days, weeks, to process all the arrests and question every suspect thoroughly. Anything unusual would be brought to his attention, but still he knew they didn't have weeks, or even days. Whoever these brazen foreign actors were, they were urgently pursuing a mission that he didn't quite understand.

"They're going after Mìng Rénshēng," he said to Minister Li, "but for what end? If it's not dissidents and not terrorists, what are they doing?"

The instant he asked the question, Shen realized one potential answer could be that they were simply trying to stop the program, and if that was true, he secretly and silently hoped they were successful. *What if their mission is to destroy the program?* he asked himself.

Li continued pulling up past cases and different suspects from his database of Western operatives, then finally found what he was looking for—a case where western tech billionaire and an unknown Chinese woman were working to block Chinese attempts to secretly manipulate the weather. He let out a grunt and a sigh, a sound Shen had only heard his boss make a few times before.

"What is it?" Shen asked.

"I think I've identified at least one of the fugitives," Li said, sounding deeply concerned rather than excited, as one might expect him to be when cracking such an important question in their most critical case.

"Who is it?"

"Chase Malone," Li said.

Shen, knowing the name, looked shocked.

"Get me everything we have on him," Li snapped as he pulled out his secure phone. "Run every image we've picked up of the fugitives through facial recognition database again, but this time tell it to compare to Chase Malone."

Chapter Forty-One

Eventually they found an old deer trail that may have also seen some limited human traffic. Chase and Wen walked through the woods on a high, narrow track of packed dirt and pine needles. For a moment, that endless, nine-inch-wide path seemed to be their entire world—a refuge from enemies, known and unknown, the ticking clock, and all the killings.

"Look," Wen said, pointing to a shimmering lake nestled in the trees. "I'd really like to clean up."

Chase knew what she wanted was to wash the blood off her hands, her arms, the splatters on her face. "No one knows where we are," he said, touching her shoulder. "I think we can risk it."

They walked halfway around the lake to a finger of water that was out of sight from the trail. They hadn't seen anyone since they'd landed, but just to be sure, they made sure they were well concealed. They both stripped down naked. Wen carefully rinsed out her clothes, which held the most blood, enough that the crystal clear water went red.

After Chase rinsed his own blood from the leg of his pants, they draped the clothes on bare branches to dry in the sun. They felt grateful that the small clearing by the shore was on the sunny side of the lake at that hour.

Wen found a fallen tree, bleached white with age, extending out into the lake, and tiptoed to the end of it. She stood there for a moment, absorbing the sun, checking the water's depth, then looked to the sky for approaching helicopters.

Chase watched her every move, savoring her beauty. Wen dove in.

"How's the water?" Chase asked as he prepared to follow her.

"Refreshing!"

"I'll take that to be a synonym for freezing cold," he said, jumping in, but was delighted to discover not only *was* it refreshing, but surprisingly warm—or at least not freezing. They swam together in the soft water, suddenly normal again, having shed the blood, the past, their identities. Wen wrapped herself around him as they bobbed near the middle of the lake, its velvet water massaging their naked bodies, the sun healing them. Chase caressed her, trying to soothe the agony of the day. "I'm sorry," he said, as their legs kicked together. His hand ran up her back and down again.

"Don't be." She kissed him again. "We're doing what we have to do."

"I know," he whispered. They held each other in silence, absorbing the tranquility, until their legs got tired and they swam back to shore. Their clothes weren't quite dry, so they found a sunny rock hidden by trees and shared an energy bar.

"How's your leg?" she asked, inspecting the wound.

"A scratch," he said, although they both knew it was worse than that. "What's it like for you being back in China?"

"It's wonderful in some ways, but at the same time, awful . . . the memories of what's gone forever, the crime of what the communists are doing to my beautiful country."

"Tell me some of the memories that will never be again," he said, finishing the bar and pointing to the empty wrapper with puppy dog eyes, raising his eyebrows.

Wen looked at him, a soft shake of her head telling him there was no more, and then her eyes went hard, defiant, suddenly a stranger, and they filled. Tears streamed down her cheeks. Uncharacteristically, she didn't fight them. Chase took her hands in his and stared into her crying eyes, wanting to absorb the emotions, her history, to take some of the pain and carry that burden for her. They stayed like that for a couple of minutes, until the tears subsided. Then she told stories of her childhood, happy times with her sister, her parents and paternal grandmother.

"Zǔ mǔ," she said softly, "is the strongest woman I've ever known. Growing up, she would show me the old ways. My Zǔ mǔ taught me how to survive in the wilderness. She showed me which plants were safe to eat, which ones could be used for healing. Zǔ mǔ told me again and again, 'This is important! My grandmother taught me, and now I'm teaching you.'"

"She sounds very special," Chase said, happy to see her now so animated and relaxed.

"Oh yes, the old ways are more and more lost now. My sister was a better student than I was."

"Is that why the MSS wanted you and your sister, because of that experience?" Chase asked.

Wen's expression turned angry again. "They wanted us

because my father was already an agent. They like generations who understand the trust. They didn't give us a choice." She barked out the words, as if trying to hit someone with them. "Just as my father had not been given a choice. He did so well in school and in the subjects they liked. Never forget, the MSS takes some of the brightest, particularly if they are also good at athletics. If not, they push them to the sciences. But the MSS recruits from there as well. At that time, we didn't think it was so bad. My father was upset they wanted us, but he could do nothing. We would have rather done other things."

"What did you want to do instead?"

"It was a good career, and we had no choice," she said, ignoring his question.

He tried again. "What were your dreams?"

She shook her head.

"Please, tell me."

She smiled bashfully, as if embarrassed. "I wanted to be a doctor."

"That's wonderful," Chase said. "You would've made a great doctor." But he knew as he said those words that it was a hard thing to hear, and now it made even more sense why killing took such a toll on her.

"Maybe one day," she said, as a single new tear fell.

Chapter Forty-Two

Later, Chase looked at Wen as they came out of an erotic embrace when his phone vibrated for attention. "Who do you think it is?" Wen asked.

"I'm willing to bet it's Tess."

"You'd be right."

"How do you think she could get this call through?"

"Three letters," Wen said. "C.I.A."

"I better take it," he said, reluctant to end their passion.

"Of course you should take it," Tess said before Chase had accepted.

"What do you mean? How did you hear us? How long have you *been* hearing us?"

"Don't worry about me listening in," Tess said. "It's the satellite photos that are the most interesting."

"Are you kidding?" Chase ran to grab their clothes.

"Don't be so modest," Tess said with a slight laugh. "Nudity should be the least of your worries right now. I don't need to remind you that you're a fugitive, essentially behind enemy lines, wanted by the entire military intelligence and law enforcement apparatus of the most controlling dictatorship on earth—"

"No, thanks, you don't need to remind us."

"Good. Because I didn't call to do that, or to interrupt your fun. We've got a lead. Perhaps a way into the central facility of Mìng Rénshēng."

"With the hidden flowers?" he asked hopefully.

"Not yet. I'm talking about the main lab, the center of the entire program—BioCheng. We have a person inside."

"One of the scientists?"

"No, one of MSS Minister Li's lieutenants. Perhaps his favorite and most trusted."

Chase looked at Wen, who was still getting dressed, while listening to the call on speaker.

"Shen Hán?" Wen asked, surprised.

"That's him," Tess said.

"I don't believe it. He would not cooperate *against* Li, against China."

"He's not exactly cooperating, but we have him under deep surveillance, and he has strong disagreements with the minister about Mìng Rénshēng."

"Strong enough to risk his life?" Wen asked.

"Possibly."

"*Possibly* isn't good enough. Our lives are on the line. I don't want to walk into another trap," Wen said defiantly, this being the first time she had openly challenged Tess so adamantly.

"I'm trying to help," Tess said, matching Wen's tone.

"Are you?" Wen asked.

"Okay, okay," Chase said, trying to calm the two women. "What do we have on this guy?"

"As I said, he is against the program, believes it is as

dangerous as we do. He's been pressing Minister Li to challenge the leadership, and—"

"Li will never challenge the leadership," Wen interrupted. "How do you have this information?"

"I'm sure it won't surprise you to hear that I'm not at liberty to reveal that."

"I know more about China, and the MSS, than you ever will," Wen said. "And I'm telling you that Shen Hán is painfully, to his core, aware that even discussing this with somebody is tantamount to signing his own death warrant." She looked up at the sky, as if trying to listen for a sound.

Chase followed her eyes, alarmed.

She shook her head, indicating it was nothing, and resumed her rant. "Minister Li understands that challenging the leadership on Mìng Rénshēng, a program this important, would be the same as ending his career. These are smart men, who know the consequences, and would not put themselves in jeopardy. So I'm asking you again, *how* have you obtained this information? We are here in the field, behind enemy lines, as you say, and if we are to go forward, I need to know the source."

Chase pursed his lips, never believing that Tess would answer the question, thought that they risked cutting off one of their best lines of information. *If Tess abandons us in China, we will be relying only on the spotty efforts of the Astronaut, and what information the now embattled Chinese WOLF members could glean*, he thought.

The silence hung heavy.

"We have Shen Hán's neighbor," Tess finally said.

Chase's face revealed his surprise, but he kept it out of his voice as he looked up at the sky, wondering if Tess had just seen his expression. "What do you mean you *have* his neighbor? You've captured him? You're interrogating him?"

"He is working for us," she clarified. "He is a wealthy businessman, with ties to United States business."

"Then the MSS would suspect him," Wen said.

"They do not suspect him. He is listening in on the conversations between Shen Hán and his wife. Pillow talk. You can learn a lot from listening to it," Tess said in a sly tone.

Chase and Wen looked at each other, certain she had been listening to them make love. Chase was angry, but was not about to let Tess know that, and there was nothing he could do about it anyway. He knew she knew he was angry. That's why she was making it clear she had been listening.

"So what does it get us just because Li's lieutenant is against the program?" Chase asked.

"We can approach him," Tess said.

"Who?" Wen asked. "Not us."

"No," Tess said, "that would be too dangerous."

"It would be too dangerous for *anybody* to approach him," Wen said harshly. "Shen Hán would have them arrested immediately."

"Not if it was his wife," Tess said.

"Oh, good God," Chase groaned. "You're going to put his *wife* against him? Is that even possible?"

"We think so."

Wen shook her head and closed her eyes. "'*We think so*' isn't good enough. *Possibly, probably, maybe*, none of these things are good enough if you're not sitting in an office in Langley, Virginia."

"I'm not in Langley."

"Wherever you are, you're not in China. You sit in a safe office with no chance of being killed, while we are out here, and they are hunting us."

"And they're getting closer every minute," Tess said. "Just remember, this was your choice."

Chapter Forty-Three

Back in his office, Minister Li stood while three technicians explained to him the different grids and anatomical breakdowns he was looking at as the most sophisticated facial recognition system in the world cycled through billions and billions of variables, reconstructing faces from data points and camera pickups from all over China.

"These correlations are supplemented by global databases," one of the men said. "As you requested, we've taken every known photo of Chase Malone and told the system to analyze them."

"So *is* this Chase Malone?" Li asked.

The three experts looked at each other, none seemingly willing to answer the question.

Li quickly grew impatient. Unlike some of his superiors, the MSS minister did not appreciate yes-men. "Somebody better have an answer."

Another quick exchange of glances between the men, and one of them spoke. "Minister, we do not know for sure, but there is a very good likelihood, or rather, it is at least *possible* that that is Chase Malone."

"I know it is *possible* that it is Chase Malone," Li said irritably. "It's *possible* that it's you, or me, or anyone! My question remains: *Is* it Chase Malone?"

The most timid looking of the three started to speak, but his voice failed him.

Li turned on him like a snake, hissing, "What is it?"

"I, I," the man stuttered. "I believe it *is* Chase Malone."

Li smiled slightly and rolled his hand, indicating he should continue.

The timid man proceeded to point out irregularities in the system's results. One of the other experts shook his head, clearly disagreeing and believing that the minister should not be bothered with such inconclusive theories. He began to speak, but Li silenced him with a wave.

"Continue," Li said to the timid man.

"I think they are trying to fool our systems."

"It is impossible to do," one of the experts objected.

"How is he doing it?" Li interrupted, already convinced that their mystery man was Chase Malone. The billionaire had long been a thorn in his side.

"It is hard to say," the man said, looking at the screens and pointing to several magnified images. "It is this cross section here and here that makes me believe it is him, or at least somebody very sophisticated who is fooling the algorithms, and you see how under high magnification, this face pixelates differently than this one. The first one is very normal based on the resolution of the camera being used to capture the image. The second one should look the same, but it does not. It blurs, and almost drips, and then it is like the computer reassembles it with the pixels in a different order. You can see how it changes." He looked at Li, now more confident. "This man does not match his face. He is an imposter."

"Is he wearing a mask?"

"Not any kind of traditional mask . . . " The timid man hesitated again.

"What?"

"It is just a theory, but look at this." He magnified another image.

The two other men began making apologies. "Sir, this is wild speculation. We know of no technology capable of—"

"I did not ask your opinion," Li snapped.

The timid man looked at Li.

"Continue," Li said.

"This is how he's doing it, I believe." The man pointed at a spot on the screen.

Li scrutinized the image, uncertain what he was looking at. "I don't understand, what is that?"

The man zoomed back out, revealing the face of the suspect again, and then zoomed back in. Under such intense magnification, it looked like a tiny gold pin in the middle of a stormy white sea.

"What is that?" Li asked again.

"I am not certain, but I believe it is a microchip."

"We do not concur," one of the other men said. "For that to be a microchip able to process information that could project, distort, or amplify any visual data which could fool our facial recognition system, it would have to be at least a decade ahead of our most advanced technology."

Li looked at the timid man. "Is that possible?"

The man nodded slowly. "The technology expands exponentially. There are secret labs all over the world. It could already exist." He looked back at the screen. "I believe it does." He magnified the screen image again and pointed to several other tiny flecks. "Look here. I think these are more."

"They are anomalies," the other expert proclaimed. "A photo magnified at that rate can show almost anything."

"There is a pattern," the timid man countered. "Anomalies do not form patterns." Zooming out and part way back in using an overlay, he connected the patterns of the flex anomalies with the original gold point, illustrating a clear geometric design. "And if I show it to you with the 3D model," he said, adjusting the projection. The pattern appeared to form a digital mask around the subject's face.

Chapter Forty-Four

Wen whispered to Chase that trusting Tess and thinking they could trust Shen Hán were like kissing two heads of the same serpent.

"Were going to try the wife," Tess said, pretending she had not heard Wen's warning. "We have reason to believe she will cooperate if she tells her husband he cannot turn her in. He's in love with her."

"How do you know he loves her that much?"

"Because we listen. Trust me, he loves her. He's not going to turn her in. The only risk is he may not do what she wants, but we think there's a better chance he will. Remember, he is completely opposed to the program."

Wen shook her head again in disgust. "And what is she going ask him to do?"

"Help us get the information. The MSS is in charge of the security, of the couriers, and the physical lab locations—including all the data. He will know how to circumvent that, to get us into BioCheng, where the information is."

"And he's going to do this because he wants to stop the program?"

"We believe so," Tess said.

"You *believe* so—here we go again!" Wen said. "The man's *whole life* has been spent fighting China's great enemy—the US imperialist Empire—and you think because he and his wife have good sex, that he's going to betray his country, and everything he has worked for his *entire life*, just because he is afraid that gene editing could get out of control? What if the *Americans* take it out of control?"

Tess sighed. "Shen Hán knows the Chinese are way ahead, and he needs the Americans to counter that. There is no oversight on the Chinese; he needs the information out. It's the same game we're playing—"

"This is not a game!" Wen shouted. "We are *killing* people. People are *dying*. People are trying to kill *us*." She quickly wiped away another lone, frustrated tear.

"Who do you think you're talking to, Wen?" Tess asked in a deadly tone. "Would you like me to tell you just how many people *you've* killed? Not just today, but this month, this year? In fact, I can get pretty close to the number of deaths you're responsible for over your entire career. I can give them to you in alphabetical order, categorized by age, nationality, geographic location of their birth, and/or death. So don't pretend that I don't know what's going on, because I can give you that same list of the deaths that *I've* been responsible for, and it's a hell of a lot bigger than yours.

"Look, I'm sorry these people had to die, but we have a job to do, don't we? And we've decided that there are bad people in the world and that we have to stop them from doing the things they do that make them bad. That's all I'm trying to do. I don't understand why you've taken such personal dislike to me when all I'm trying to do is keep the two of you alive and help you complete your mission—one that you *voluntarily* walked into. Hell, you called *me*, remember?"

"Wen is just increasingly on edge since coming back to China, I'm sure you understand," Chase interjected. "These are her people, the good and the bad, and this is a very difficult situation. We appreciate your help, but Tess, you must know . . . we don't *trust* you."

"Of course I know you don't trust me, but I'm the best shot you have of getting out of the country alive. And Chase, you must know, *we* don't trust *you*."

"We'll take our chances," Wen said.

"That would be a mistake," Tess shot back.

"Let me ask you something then," Wen said, looking into the phone as if she could see Tess in her cushy, non-Langley office. "*Should* we trust you?"

After a long silence, Tess replied, "That reminds me of a riddle. You come to a fork in the road. A sign tells you that one road leads to paradise, the other leads to an apocalyptic land. There are two brothers guarding the roads. The sign also tells you that one of them always lies, and the other one always tells the truth. You can ask only one question, to only one of the brothers, to figure out which road leads to paradise. What do you ask?"

"What does this have to do with anything?" Wen asked.

"You ask one of them what his brother would say is the road to Paradise," Chase said. "If it is the liar, he will say my brother will tell you that one is the road, and it won't be true, so it will be the other one. If it is the truth-teller, knowing his brother would lie, he will tell you what his brother would say, and, once again, you will know it is the other road."

"Correct," Tess said, impressed with Chase's quick response.

"You didn't answer my question," Wen said.

"No, I didn't. However, if you insist, I will. But you must understand the business we are all in."

"So that's a no?" Wen asked. "We should not trust you?"

"Correct," Tess said. "As a rule, you should not trust me. Yet sometimes you have to. And now is one of those times."

Chase looked at Wen. They held each other's gaze for a moment. She was fiery angry. Hoping to soothe her, he took her hand stroked one of her fingers. "Call us back once you know if the wife's on board, and if you get anything, " Chase said. "We appreciate it."

"Will do."

"Oh, and one more thing," Chase said. "How close is the MSS right now? Are we going to be able to make it to BioCheng?"

"You two have proven pretty resourceful. I think you're safe for the moment, and will probably make it to safety this evening. What you have to be worried about is tomorrow."

"Tomorrow?"

"Minister Li is unleashing all the fury of hell upon you, and his wrath is unmerciful."

Chapter Forty-Five

The tension in Li's office intimidated the three data experts, but exhilarated the minister.

"Okay . . . I'm convinced that man has found a way to trick our systems," Li said. "That sounds like something Chace Malone would both be capable of, and would do. What I want to know is can you prove to me it is him?"

"If you capture him," one of the other men said.

Li glared at him.

"I believe so," the timid man said. "But I have to write a new program specifically aimed at analyzing, in much greater depth and resolution, Chase Malone's face in photographic history. Videos will help, and then I will feed it all in with the 3D overlays, and I think we can find those original patterns conforming to his face and create a match. If it's him, we'll know."

"How long do you need?"

"Twenty-four hours."

"Make it twelve, and you've got a deal. If you do it in six hours, you've got a promotion."

The timid man bowed, immediately leaving the room without even glancing at his two co-workers.

"You are dismissed as well," Li said to them.

"What about the woman?" one of them asked.

"She is Chinese. Perhaps Malone, or whoever he is, is connected to one of the dissident groups and she is his contact for local intelligence."

None of the three men in the room believed that, but the other two were not in a position to question the minister.

"She does not show up in any of our databases."

Of course, the minister already knew this. It had been bothering him ever since the two fugitives burst onto the scene. She didn't match. If she was a Chinese national, they would have her.

"She's wearing a digital mask as well," Li said.

The other men nodded, but still weren't convinced. An awkward silence followed.

"But if she's wearing a digital mask, who is she?" one of them asked.

"Then can you find her?"

"Is she more important than Chase Malone?"

The minister wanted to say no, but he nodded slowly. There was something grave, something sinister about this woman. He had tracked Malone once before with a Chinese woman, and he'd been beaten by them. She was special.

"You find out who she is, and depending on who she is, you will be appropriately rewarded."

They smiled, relieved.

"Now go, and do not come back until you can answer that question."

Once the men were gone, Li made a mental note that as

soon as the timid man came back with a positive ID on Chase Malone, he would assign him to identify the Chinese woman, believing he would be more likely to find her than the other two "experts."

His assistant sent in his next appointment. The short, portly man walked in carrying several thick black folders and a large laptop computer, and quickly spread it all on a table. "Minister, if you're ready, I can tell you everything you need to know about Chase Malone."

"Excellent. But before you begin, the most important thing I'd like to know about Malone is where is he right now. Do you think you can tell me that?"

"Perhaps," the man said with a kind of scholarly confidence that Li liked.

The man pushed his thick eyeglasses up. "A man's life, his actions, his travels, his friends and associates, tell a very detailed story about him. And it leads to one place."

The minister looked at the man expectantly, asking the question with his eyes.

The man licked his lips, clicked the computer on, and opened one of the black folders. "I am sure once you see the story of Malone's life, you will conclude, as I have, that he could only be in one place today, and that is China."

Chapter Forty-Six

Chase and Wen reached the village. "We're lucky," she said, pointing to a cell tower. "Many towns this size do not have cell coverage."

She reached Mei Lein, who informed her that the repercussions against WOLF and others had already begun.

"I'm sorry."

"We've taken precautions," Mei Lein said. "We have plans in place for this."

"Of course," Wen said, knowing that sooner or later, The Cause would have exposed itself to the party's fury. "Can we help?"

"It's best you don't know our plans." Mei Lein gave her some additional information they had just received about the labs.

At the same time, Chase managed to get ahold of the Astronaut. Chase asked him about the courier's information. The Astronaut confirmed what Chase had already suspected: if they wanted the core data of the program, they would have to go into BioCheng to get it.

"A suicide mission," the Astronaut said.

Wen arranged a ride to the next city—only an hour away, and it had a high-speed rail terminal.

While they rode in the back of a truck, Chase gave her a rundown of his conversation with the Astronaut. "First, of course, he was sorry not to speak with you, and wanted to remind you that he strongly recommends we leave China now."

She smiled.

"But he was able to take the information we had on the lab locations, combine it with the courier's data, and feed it into his system. It's not much, but it's all we've got. We have to go into BioCheng."

"We'll never get through the MSS security," Wen said.

"That's what he said. But they'll think we're going to where the courier was headed. Hopefully that'll give us a seam to go through. If we get really lucky, they'll think we're dead in a plane crash."

"The MSS will be on that wreckage pretty quick, and will discover no bodies."

"Too bad we didn't plan it. We could've taken a couple of those MSS agents from the fitness center and left them on the plane."

She made a face, as if his whole comment was unnecessary and inappropriate.

"Sorry. We have to get into BioCheng."

She nodded reluctantly. "Then we can leave China."

"We need Tess or the Astronaut to find the missing children."

"If . . . "

"If the hidden flowers are real . . . and alive."

"Do you really think we *need* them?" Wen asked. "Are you just wanting to save them?"

"Both," Chase admitted. "Children suffering is something I don't appreciate, and if I can do something about it, I'm going to."

"Risky."

"That said, having living, breathing examples of what the Chinese government has done is also pretty compelling, and I think we need to go there. That's where the true records are."

"If it's even real."

"It's real."

She nodded knowing full well it was.

"And hopefully at BioCheng we'll get some records that give us more insights to where they are. Tess may come up empty on that."

"Did you remind the Astronaut?"

"I did. He's still searching."

The driver dropped them off a few blocks from the train station. They found a secluded spot to reapply their vIDs. "Let's hope your invention is as brilliant as you are," Wen said. "It's more important than ever that this works. I'm sure they've got every camera within a thousand miles of the ghost city looking for us."

"Remember, the people they're looking for died in a plane crash," Chase said. "We're somebody entirely different now. And they're not going to find us."

As they walked to the station, they counted a dozen cameras, plus four more capturing the entrance.

Chapter Forty-Seven

Wen watched everyone on the train with the subtle skill of a super-spy. They waited to be recognized, and kept clear of cameras as best they could. Their only weapons were a pistol, a knife, and a grenade. A gray-haired woman and a bald man sat diagonally across the aisles from them. Wen saw wedding rings, and decided they were a couple. The only other people near them were two young women in their twenties.

"My sister and I took this train often," Wen said, so quietly that Chase wasn't sure if she was talking to herself, or to him.

"I know she died, but you never told me how."

Their eyes met, hers like a little girl, afraid, ashamed. She shook her head slowly, as if she couldn't face a conversation about those memories right now.

Chase pressed, because he thought it would be good for her to talk about it, especially while they were in China. "Please?"

Wen looked back at the young women, then to Chase. "We were going to leave together."

"Home? The MSS? Or China?"

"All of it. We were leaving together."

"What happened?"

"Rong Lo happened." Wen touched Chase's hand.

"Rong Lo," Chase said bitterly, thinking of the man who'd pursued them both when they were first reunited.

"Rong Lo was more than just my superior," Wen said. "He was . . . in love with me."

Chase was surprised at the revelation.

"I did not return his affection. He was a cold and bitter man. Even in my days of having loyalty to the MSS, I had no interest in him whatsoever." She appeared angry, her voice shaky. "Rong Lo discovered our plot to leave, and he found out where we would be meeting. One of our friends turned us in. She had no choice. They were torturing her family." Wen looked out the window. "We didn't know we'd been betrayed. Rong Lo went to the meeting, but at the last minute I received a warning from my sister not to come because she saw him coming with a group of men. I was still fifteen minutes away and, of course, I rushed there to try to save her, but by the time I got there, she was dead."

Wen turned back to Chase. He expected to see tears in her eyes, but there was fire instead.

"Rong Lo and the others were waiting. There was a trap. I wanted to kill them all, but there were too many, and I was too upset, and even in that state, I went back to my training, which told me never to fight with emotions."

"I'm sorry," Chase said. He put his arm around her, their foreheads pressed together.

"He killed my sister," she said through gritted teeth, as if it had just happened.

Chase couldn't imagine getting that close to saving his brother, Boone, only to see his killers with fresh blood on their hands and not being able to do anything about it. Rong Lo had made a mistake in coming after them, but Chase wondered if they'd made a similar mistake in coming back to China.

Li and Shen had moved downstairs to the Crisis Center to better monitor the escalating situation. A man in a military uniform burst breathlessly into the room. Li looked at him with disdain.

"The plane," the man began. "The plane is empty."

"Repeat that," Li said, as if injured.

"We got a Zone-slicer up there. It's a plane designed to monitor and probe—"

"I know what it does!"

"Yes, well, we used heat readings and x-ray technologies . . . there is no one on that plane."

"Where did they go, then?" Li asked, trying to hide his panic and rage.

"They must have jumped out before the fighters showed up," Shen offered.

The military man nodded his agreement.

"The fighters were over their wings in thirteen minutes," Li said. "The helicopters had them for five of those minutes. The fighters would have had a visual a minute before arriving. That's a seven minute window. Draw it up! Find out where they dropped in those seven minutes. Find them!"

Chapter Forty-Eight

Wen looked at the older couple and the young women again. They didn't appear interested in them.

"Is your grandmother the last relative you have left in China?" Chase asked, still speaking quietly so they could not be overheard.

"Yes. Zǔ mǔ is all I have, and yet I don't have her."

"How is she allowed to remain?"

"Once we erased the MSS records of my existence, and my sister and father were dead, they could not trace her to a defector. She was just an old lady with no family."

"Do you want to see her?"

"I would love to see her, to hug Zǔ mǔ again . . . but it is too risky for her. She is nearly seventy, and she is safe. If we went to see her, just to make me happy, somebody could follow us, find her . . . "

"There must be a way."

"We're in too much trouble now. And not just our old trouble, this is a whole new world of trouble." She looked at the other passengers again. He could see that she was lost in memories.

"Would it make her happy to see you?"

"Of course, it would make her very happy. We were so close. She has no family left either—but it is too risky, we cannot do it." Wen shot him one of her 'end-of-discussion' looks.

Chase nodded.

"When they killed my father, Zǔ mǔ suffered greatly. He was her only son. She believed he was the sparkle in the sun's rays."

Chase had heard bits and pieces of the story of her father's death before, but never all of it. "Your dad?"

She was quiet for a while before she finally began. "He discovered a program in which the MSS was arresting and torturing dissidents before sending them to slave labor camps. It was very secret, but some of the ones he had arrested were sent there, and it always bothered him to charge people whose only crime was disagreeing with the government. These individuals weren't plotting to overthrow or anything like that, they simply disagreed with policies. In America, those same ones could be running for office themselves, or on television, sharing their views, but in China, they were tortured for names, and then sent away forever to slave labor camps—which weren't even supposed to exist."

"What did your father do?"

"He could not go to his supervisors because they would simply demote him, or punish him in other ways, perhaps even send my sister and I to work in factories, but he also could not sleep. It was impossible for him to bear, so he studied, and he found out who in authority would be the most sympathetic because he did not believe this program was sanctioned by the entire government, but rather created and run solely by the MSS. It was corruption. Slave labor benefited few people. He found the man he thought could help in the government. A critic of the MSS."

"Are people *allowed* to criticize the MSS?"

"Sometimes, carefully, certain important high-ranking authorities can question or offer guidance—very softly, very gently. But this man had pushed it several times, not publicly, but privately enough that when my father went looking for someone, everything pointed to this man, Mengyao."

"Did your father tell Mengyao?"

"Yes, he went and told him." Wen stared out the window for a moment as the countryside blurred past.

"What happened?"

"Mengyao listened very carefully. He took many notes, then he thanked my father, actually congratulated him for being brave, and promised he would see to the matter as best he could. Mengyao warned my father, for his own sake, not to tell anyone else, not to discuss it again."

"Did Mengyao do something?"

"My father came home that night and told my mother everything. She was very concerned. For months he had been upset about something, but hadn't told her for fear of endangering us. My mother was worried that he had gone to Mengyao."

"Did he tell you?"

"No. My sister and I were already in the MSS. He would've put us in great danger." She stopped and watched one of the two young women tapping the screen on her phone. "My mother told me all of this later." She paused, trying to contain her emotions. "I don't know what Mengyao did, but the next day, my father was dead."

"How?"

Her face filled with anger, tears dropping down her cheeks. "A bullet to the back of his head. They shot my beautiful father in the back of the head because they were afraid to give him a chance to defend himself. The cowards."

Chase tried to hold her.

"No. Being back in China, it is all I can do not to go visit Mengyao and put a bullet in the back of *his* head."

Chapter Forty-Nine

The train slowed. "This is our stop," Wen said suddenly.

Chase, knowing it wasn't their stop, picked up the urgency in her tone and followed her off the train.

"Come on," she said, sliding into the moving swell of travelers inside the busy terminal. A few minutes later, they were on the street.

"What's going on?" Chase asked, trying to catch his breath as they jogged into an alley.

"Those two women on the train are MSS agents."

"Are you sure?" He rarely questioned her on such matters, but wondered if she'd been projecting her sister and herself on the women.

"Yes. They got an alert on their phone to be on the lookout for us, and were about to make a move." She ducked around a corner and came to a small courtyard that appeared to lead to a school of some sort.

"Do you think they followed us?"

Wen, counting silently to herself, did not answer.

Chase realized that the women were coming. He hadn't

heard them yet, but he could tell by her face that she was expecting combat.

Wen handed Chase the pistol. "Hopefully you won't . . ."

Suddenly, she leaped onto a low wall, ran along its narrow top, and then jumped off and disappeared.

Chase ran back the way they'd come, trying to get to her. By the time he arrived twenty-some seconds later, Wen was dragging the body of one of the women into the courtyard. The other laid nearby, lifeless.

"Bring her," Wen yelled quietly.

"Is she dead?"

"No, just unconscious."

Chase was not surprised, after all the talk about Wen and her sister as MSS agents, that she would try not to kill these two. He put the woman next to the other one where Wen had hidden them behind a large decorative shrub.

"Let's go," Wen said, scrolling through the woman's phone.

Three vehicles later, including a crowded bus that Chase didn't believe would have been licensable back in the States, they were within walking distance of a WOLF safe house. However, after a hasty call to Mei Lein, an old, dirty box truck picked them up. They rode, locked inside the closed cargo with a pallet of smelly, colorful plastic, for several miles before being "delivered" to a safe house.

The building, like the majority of WOLF hideouts, was a small commercial warehouse and actually an ongoing enterprise. In one half of the building small toys and other plastic things were packaged for western consumers, few of whom would ever ponder the places and people at the products' origins. Trucks pulled up to the loading docks, bringing in components and taking out finished products, most bound for America. A separate section of offices housed a residential area where Angúo and three other WOLF operatives were waiting.

"I'm so happy to see you still alive and well," Angúo said, smiling as if he'd just received a wonderful gift.

The truck that had brought them there was driven by a member of the resistance who did not know the full extent of WOLF's operations, nor the importance of his passengers, and definitely not that they would be staying there. China was a complex society with many factions of dissidents—from the simple protesters to full-fledged revolutionaries—and it was the young people who fueled the greatest dissent, as was almost always the case throughout history. The differing groups did not always agree with each other, but they definitely shared a common enemy: the Communist Party and the ruling elite. Yet, as with everything in China, those lines were complex and often blurred, particularly once the local government was brought into the picture.

"It's gotten bad since you hit the courier," Angúo said. "They've arrested thousands."

"Thousands of *WOLF* members?" Chase asked, surprised there were that many Chinese in the secretive organization.

"No. We are not the largest resistance organization, but we are the most well-funded, organized, and secret. Still, we have lost more than fifty so far. Tonight will be worse. Tomorrow . . . I don't even want to think about."

"It's because of us," Wen said, pacing in the space that was more like an Army barrack.

"No," Angúo said. "You know better. The crackdown is because of the movement. There is risk whenever we take action."

"You are risking your life for us," Wen said.

"It is an honor. A debt I am grateful to pay," Angúo said.

Wen looked at him closely. "It's you."

He nodded.

"What?" Chase asked.

"My sister, she . . ."

"She saved my life," Angúo said. "She . . . I owe her everything."

"My sister fell in love with a man. It turned out he was in the resistance, but neither of them knew what the other did. By the time she found out, he was on an arrest list. She could not save him." Wen looked at Angúo as if he were a brother. "Before his execution, he got word to her to please help his lifelong friend . . ."

"Angúo?" Chase asked.

"Yes," Angúo said. "I was also on the arrest list. I would have been executed."

"My sister got to him hours before the raid."

"All the others were . . . they are all gone now."

Wen hugged him. They both shed tears, thinking of her sister.

"We must get this done," Wen said. "If we expose Míng Rénshēng, it will hurt the rulers, maybe enough to give WOLF and the others a chance to stop them."

"The only way to stop them is to win," Angúo agreed.

"We'll go into the lab tonight," Chase said.

"It's not just the lab," a woman said. "It is the Hidden Flowers."

"Forget about the children," another man said, admonishing her. "We don't know where they are, or even if they are real."

"We know!" the woman argued.

"The children will do no good," the man insisted.

"I think she's right," Chase said. "The children could change everything."

"How?" the man asked. "When you expose the BioCheng, you will slow and give the international community a chance to monitor China's program."

They went in and out of Mandarin and broken English, with Wen translating for Chase when necessary.

"But you will not bring down the regime," the woman said, looking at all their faces carefully before continuing, as if knowing she was committing another level of treason. "To change the regime, there is only one way to do that. You must get the people on your side, and not just WOLF, not just the other dissidents. You must have the masses behind the revolution. Once all the people see what the government did to children, it will be different."

"The communist government has exploited children forever," the man said. "Why would a handful of children born from a science experiment be any different?"

"It is true," she agreed. "Sadly, we have let the government get away with too much—hurting our children, making them work, arresting them, stealing their parents, killing the baby girls—but this is different. These children had no chance. And it is not just them, but all their children's children, on and on forever. Humanity's future."

The man tried to interrupt, but Chase asked him to let her finish.

"They are the living example, the innocence, and truth, that will be stolen forever."

"The government is on the brink of intervening with

natural evolution," Angúo added. "The consequences, as you know, are dire, perhaps leading to extinction, and they are irreversible."

"And in the children's innocent eyes, the people will see that bleak future being forced upon us," the woman said. "They will see and understand what the government is risking in order to achieve their objectives."

"Where do we find the children?" Chase asked.

"After the lab," Wen said.

"We can do both," Chase said. "We *must* do both."

Angúo moved back the curtain and looked out the window. "I'm afraid there won't be time."

Chapter Fifty

Minister Li walked into the ornate room, and although respected, and even feared among many of those gathered, in this meeting, he was not the ultimate superior. At the head of the long, black, polished table, the president of China sat with an unreadable expression. Seated down the sides, the upper party officials also wore stoic faces. Li had rarely been in this position, and did not like it, yet he felt no intimidation.

"How did this happen?" the president asked him in an uncharacteristically open and forceful manner. Normally one of his deputies would begin this line of questioning. It showed Li what he already knew—that nothing was more important to the party than the Míng Rénshēng program and discovering the identities of whomever had breached it.

"I believe the man leading this attack is Chase Malone, an American."

"CIA?" one of the other men asked.

"We do not believe the operation is sanctioned by the

CIA. However, he may be receiving information or assistance from them."

"Who is this man?" the president asked in a tone a god might use when talking about an annoying mortal.

"Malone is an American tech engineer, a billionaire. A little over a year ago he disappeared, and has rarely been seen since." Without checking his notes, Li went on to give more detail about Chase's background, including his time spent studying in China.

"What is his interest here?"

"It appears he is simply against what we are doing with Mìng Rénshēng."

"He is an American," another man said. "Surely he seeks to profit from this, and get beyond where we are?"

"I don't believe so," Li said.

"But you do not know," another man said.

"Not yet, but we will," Li responded in an icy tone.

The president liked Minister Li, and trusted him as much as he could afford to trust anyone who might one day take his job, or assist somebody else in taking his job. Yet he believed Li was loyal, and competent. The president also understood that it was impossible to be successful all the time, particularly in intelligence and counterintelligence.

"Why hasn't he been apprehended, and who is the woman he is traveling with?" the president asked.

"He has developed a way to defeat our facial recognition systems. Malone is one of the world's leading experts in artificial intelligence and machine learning computer programs."

"And the woman?" the president asked again.

"She may be the key," Li admitted. "We have not unlocked her yet."

Chase pressed Angúo and the other WOLF members about obtaining additional information on the whereabouts of the Yĭn Huāshù children.

"If the children ever existed, by now they've certainly all been killed," the defiant man insisted. "The government would never risk leaving that kind of living evidence around."

"He may be right," Angúo said. "Especially after the courier."

Chase worried their actions might have brought harm to the children. He had to admit to himself there was something more than just wanting them for the ultimate proof. Although he wouldn't realize it for some time, he needed to save the hidden flowers because he had not been there to save Wen as a child.

In spite of their differences, they each promised to pursue their leads and contacts in an effort to come up with something conclusive. In the meantime, preparations for the risky assault on BioCheng commenced.

Chase and Wen found a few moments alone while Angúo went to receive a weapons delivery and complete tasks of his own.

"You are too attached to rescuing the children," Wen said. "If they were alive yesterday, Minister Li would certainly have ordered them to be put to death today, after the courier."

"I know."

"We need to move on BioCheng."

"I think we should wait on the lab," Chase said as Wen scanned MSS messages on one of the phones from the agents on the train.

"Because you want to wait to hear from Tess?"

"Absolutely. If she really can turn Shen Hán and get us that information, it will increase the odds of our success dramatically."

"It'll be a trap," Wen said, not looking up from the agent's phone. "Not necessarily even from Tess. It could be that Li and Hán are making her people believe he's going to turn."

"What if you're wrong?"

"Okay, imagine that Hán *is* serious, and wants to sabotage Míng Rénshēng, but then he realizes it will cost him everything, so he gets scared. What's he going to do? Not just call it off. He'll make himself a hero bringing the whole chain down."

"Don't you think Tess will take all that into account?" Chase asked. "Think what you want about her, but she's a very smart woman."

"She's a smart woman in the United States, but she doesn't know China. She doesn't know how Chinese people think."

"But—"

"The MSS is *not* the CIA."

"You might be underestimating the CIA."

"I don't think we're going to have the luxury of a decision anyway," Wen said, looking up from the agent's phone. "We have to go in tonight, whether we hear from her or not."

Chapter Fifty-One

The Chinese president gulped water, realizing this threat was more serious than he'd previously thought. More than Mìng Rénshēng was at stake—China's global supremacy, and even his role as its leader, could be in jeopardy if these two 'intruders' weren't stopped.

"So you're telling us," a PLA general began, "that these people are wandering around inside our country and they are *invisible* to us?" The general punctuated his question with an incredulous expression.

"For the moment," Li replied. "However, I believe we will be able to unmask them soon."

"You believe, but you are not certain," another man said.

"No, I am not certain. I am in the intelligence business, and until I have the facts, I will not speculate and theorize. Based on my experience, which is vast in these areas, I believe we will confirm their identities within hours." Li was careful to keep his tone less severe than his words. "Yet I will not stand here and tell you that we will unmask them at a specific time, and that we know exactly who and what they are, until I know, because that is the nature of the intelligence business."

"And the woman?" the president asked again.

Li had dreaded the question. There were no good answers. All his theories pointed back to one thing, a great embarrassment, a great failure. He looked the president in the eye. "She is Chinese. We have nothing on her in our system." It was the truth, but a very incomplete truth.

The president seemed to sense something amiss in Li's response. He'd grown accustomed to hearing theories from the minister in the absence of conclusive facts, yet in this case, where there should have been numerous guesses as to her identity, none were forthcoming. The president pressed. "Is she a Chinese citizen, or is she American?"

"We are still trying to determine her actual identity."

The president nodded, making a mental note to have a private conversation with his MSS chief after the meeting.

The men continued to question the minister about the risk to Míng Rénshēng, and what information the courier had been carrying. Li gave satisfactory responses and explained what resources had been utilized to capture the fugitives. The minister assured them that everything was being done to avoid another breach, but he stopped short of guaranteeing that there would not be one. "If the CIA or some other agency is involved, we cannot know how far they have gone, and if this is worth antagonizing us, for some of these countries, including the United States, then—"

"An act of war?" the general asked.

"Why would this be?" another asked.

"Many people question the ethics of the Míng Rénshēng, and believe we are putting humanity at risk."

Several around the conference table scoffed.

"How do you feel about this?" the president asked Li.

"My opinion is not important. What matters is what you have decided, and I will use everything within my power, and that of the Ministry of State Security, to make sure that your agenda is advanced, and your decisions are carried out to the letter."

The president nodded and smiled, but it was the smile of a man who'd asked for a truthful answer and received a prepackaged one meant to appease him. He stared at the minister and made an additional note of another question for their private meeting.

"What assistance has this," one of the men checked his notes before continuing, "Chase Malone been given from locals, other than the woman he is with?"

Li went into detail about how they had begun rounding up dissidents and anybody with questionable loyalties.

"Does this warrant such a significant crackdown?" the same man asked. Everyone in the room knew that they had initiated the biggest such show of force domestically since Tiananmen Square, the 1989 months long student-led demonstrations that involved more than a million people, until the Communist government declared martial law and sent tanks and assault-rifle armed troops to end the movement. Thousands had been killed, even more injured.

"We've never had this deep an insertion into China, and they have to be getting local help," the general began. "I believe the risk is great, and definitely requires a full-force response."

"I'm certain the situation will be escalating in the hours and days to come," another man added.

"That is enough for now. We will receive another briefing from Minister Li tomorrow," the president said.

In the hall, the general stopped Li, and the two discussed the events surrounding the fugitive's plane escape from the ghost city for several minutes. Another minister intercepted Li before he could get to the elevator, asking about the national alerts that had been issued to find the fugitives.

Finally back to his car, happy to be free from the oversight, Minister Li was looking forward to returning to his office and getting the job done. His driver opened the back door for him and, as Li stepped to get in, found the president already inside, waiting. Li took a deep breath and got in beside him. The chauffeur stayed outside.

Chapter Fifty-Two

Sitting in the back seat of Li's black Hongqi limousine, China's president looked at the minister. "You have reservations about the Mìng Rénshēng program?"

"I fear Mìng Rénshēng can easily get out of control." He maintained eye-contact with the president. "It may already be out of control. I believe Chase Malone is acting alone to stop the program because he thinks it is potentially catastrophic."

"Upon what do you base your ideas?"

"As you know, MSS provides security, and several of our top people, although committed to securing the program, worry that we are going too fast, and we don't have a full understanding or even a partial understanding of the ramifications of the changes we make."

"Could some of these top MSS officials have compromised the security?"

"There is no evidence of that."

"I'm not asking about evidence."

"It is possible, but I don't believe it."

The president nodded. "Who is the woman?"

"It is true that we do not know yet," Li began. "However, we encountered Chase Malone once before, when he was trying to stop our efforts at weather control. At that time, he was also working with a Chinese woman. I believe she is the same one. She is the clue that led me to believe it might be Malone."

"If you don't know who she is, why are you so bothered by this?"

"I think there is a chance she is a former MSS agent." As he said the words, a sharp pain pinched his gut.

The president, known for his poker face, could not hide his surprise. "Then she should be easy to identify."

"Our database was compromised."

"How?" the president asked, clearly surprised again, but this time the shock on his face was not evident. "And why was I not informed of this alarming incident?"

"I've only just become aware of it today," Li said, hoping the president would believe him. "We took surveillance video of the woman with Malone, both in the United States and Mexico, and compiled everything we have of the woman with him in China. They appear to be the same person. Then we built a profile on her. She fits every profile and manner of a trained MSS agent."

"Does she match an agent?"

"There are no matches anywhere, yet her skills are so evident that based on reports of our agents and other data, including satellite images and surveillance cameras, etcetera, I am almost certain she was trained MSS. I put our experts on it, we went looking for her, and it is then that we discovered a breach through Ghost Dragon."

The president once again hid his concern, but voiced it. "So let me see if I have this right. We have a rogue former

MSS agent, who has defected, somehow accessed Ghost Dragon, manipulated the program, turned it against us, and deleted her entire profile—her very existence—from the system, and now she is working with an American billionaire—a tech genius, as you called him—who's already caused harm to our weather controlling programs, and now is trying to destroy our most important scientific program."

"Yes, sir. You understand why I did not bring this up in the meeting."

"They would have insisted I fire you. This has all happened on your watch. Most of them hate you anyway."

"Yes, sir." The minister looked at the president with a humbled expression. "I will, of course, resign immediately, if that is your wish."

"I will have no choice but to demand your resignation if you do not stop Chase Malone and apprehend the woman."

"I understand."

"If any more breaches occur, the trouble will increase—for both of us," the president said. "I do believe in you, Li. And I cannot think of anyone better suited for this job." He got out of the car.

"Thank you," Li said, relieved the encounter was over.

The president leaned back in, stared hard at the minister, and added in a firm whisper, "But . . . You. Must. Not. Fail."

Chapter Fifty-Three

Wen saw that thousands were being arrested. Hundreds had already been killed. She wanted to go into BioCheng and leave, but Chase still insisted that they needed to rescue the children.

She walked alone inside among tall rows of boxes near one of the loading docks, and did what she often did when she was upset: she called the Astronaut. She knew Chase would do anything for her, but they were often too close to objectively see each other's concerns. The Astronaut, with his calm assurance and seemingly one-dimensional personality, saw the logic in everything. A savant, who didn't like to be touched, whose strange and dry humor occurred rarely, and was a socially awkward man, yet she didn't see him that way. To Wen, he was a special, magical being, a kind of shooting star, walking on earth. From the moment they had met, he had taken to her in a special way, and for reasons she still didn't understand, he loved her.

She brightened at his voice. "I'm glad you called," he

said. "I have information that might help you—assuming you are still intent on staying where you are not safe."

"We plan to leave tomorrow," she said. "What do you have?"

"You first. You called for a reason."

"You've already answered that," she said. "I just needed a friendly voice."

"Are you okay?"

"Yes."

He said nothing for a few seconds, as if trying to think of a response. "I used all the data from the courier and was able to access Ghost Dragon."

"And?"

"All indications are that there were children."

"Were?" she echoed, surprised by how sad the past-tense made her.

"The data suggests that they may still be alive."

"Do you know where?"

"There are three possible locations. Perhaps they were kept at housing facilities, research centers, or experimental laboratories at some point. They may all be closed. However, it looks like three are still operational."

"How current is this?"

"Real time."

"Now?" she asked, even more surprised. "The MSS hasn't closed them, executed . . . "

"It appears something, or some*one*, is keeping them too busy to bother with some forgotten kids."

"Us?"

"Yes. The danger you are in is quite overwhelming."

"What is your assessment?"

"There is little chance you will make it out of China."

"I wasn't asking about us." Wen shivered at his prediction. "I meant your assessment of the hidden flowers. Are they really alive?"

"I have no feelings one way or another about it, but the data definitely suggests they are alive, and the most likely location is the Jang House."

"How many children are there?"

"There's only one reference in the information that would lead to any conclusion. The data is thin. However, I anticipated your question, and used a fundamental ratings program to create a reasonable predictive numeral. Unfortunately, it's not very specific. It would seem that you are looking for somewhere between five and twenty." He sounded embarrassed not to have a definitive number.

Wen had worried that there could be hundreds or even thousands of children who'd been experimented on, so she took this as good news. China didn't do anything in a small way, and they believed in large data sets. It was one of the reasons they were leading the world on artificial intelligence and machine learning, because those required massive amounts of data to feed the algorithms, and nobody could provide more of that than a country with 1.6 billion people.

"That's very helpful," she said. "Is there a way you can help us get to Jang House?"

"I don't think that is a very wise thing to do."

"We have to, we need the proof."

"What you need is to find out which genes they are editing, and why. The December 2018 twin girls were a good experiment in public relations, even though it didn't go over well. The hope was to eliminate the future of one of the world's most dreaded diseases—HIV—particularly when it is passed on from parents to children. Obviously, they mismanaged the information, the data, the release, and now we know they have been doing a great deal more, but it stirred the world."

"What has that to do with now?"

"Everything. It was a distraction. The information that needs to be obtained is which genes they are targeting, and why," he repeated.

"I'm confused . . . exactly what does that tell us?" Wen asked.

Chase was in the shower, having awakened from a nap. She continued looking out a high window in the warehouse, having climbed to an upper catwalk rigged around ventilation ducts, lighting, and wiring. She watched for the inevitable MSS raid. She had three guns now that WOLF had resupplied her. Wen would never go quietly.

"We need to know if it is too late," the Astronaut said firmly.

"Too late? For what?" she asked.

"The children are one thing, and remember there may be twenty, but there could be a whole other section that wasn't reported in any of the courier data. I had to dig deep and extrapolate wide to even find the shreds of information we have. It took much sorting through archives. There is a chance there could be hundreds of children, and a worse chance that there could be thousands of adults, at the other facilities. They may have begun destroying them . . . and these altered 'people' could already be mixing into the gene pool. And not just in China, because—"

"China may have weaponized the genes?" Wen interrupted. She'd assumed all along that China's quest for a master race was their endgame, but of course they could accelerate that superiority if they diluted and contaminated the gene pool in other countries. Many Americans married Chinese that they met while studying or working in related industries. *China never thinks about the short-term, they always think millennia,* she thought. "Could it have already begun?" she asked, more determined than ever to get into BioCheng, and now believing they needed to get to the children. They had to know how far it had gone in humans.

"That is why you must find out which genes and why."

"There *must* be records somewhere that you can access," she said.

"That's why they have the couriers."

"The answers are in BioCheng." She secretly wished that Tess could send two or three IT-Squads to blow open the lab for them, so she and Chase could steal the data and then get out of China, but she knew that could start an irreversible course toward World War III, and then the gene pool might not even matter anymore.

"I'll see if I can get back into Ghost Dragon and search through MSS black files for Mìng Rénshēng details, but you can imagine I won't be able to reach the up-to-date information—and after the trouble you two have created, they will have everything locked down and triple secured."

"Thank you."

"Wen, you should get out now. We can turn everything over to the CIA, let them decide what to do. They have operatives in the country."

"Not many," Wen said.

"*Not many*, says the former MSS agent. More than you might believe."

"I can't leave yet."

"I know. Then just promise me that you won't get killed."

"I can't do that either."

"I know."

Chapter Fifty-Four

Ping, a skinny twenty year-old student, sat keying in details about an upcoming secret resistance rally. She believed she was making a difference, that their cause could be victorious. The information was on an unauthorized and underground server that students used to plan rallies and other secret meetings. Their movement had been gaining ground since the recent protests in Hong Kong over an Anti-Extradition Law, which grew into on-going demonstrations about mainland China's government overreach and the demand for democratic reforms.

Ping's mother's sing-song voice, ultra-positive attitude, and tendency toward flowing pastel colored clothing, gave her the presence of a fairy princess—at least that's what her class of eight-year-olds thought. She'd been a teacher since before Ping was born, very patient and wise, able to handle a clever daughter who poked into business not necessarily her own, yet it fused them in a bond that fueled each other's energy. Her father worked in a factory, but at night she'd see his light burning too long, studying for a hospital job. Ping was proud of them, even though their lives had been too hard, especially with China's growing wealth and world power.

Ping's pixie cut black hair, fine facial features, and piercing dark eyes gave her a child-like appearance that belied her rebellious heart. She and her fellow students braced for trouble, since recent word had swept across the country, especially in the universities, that an MSS courier had been intercepted and relieved of his data. It was a brazen attack, enough to incite the revolutionaries that the all-powerful state and its MSS attack dogs were not invincible.

Her group had a big meeting planned. Ping's boyfriend, Quan, was also part of the movement, and often spoke of freedom and elections of choice at their gatherings. He inspired people, especially her. In private, they spoke of one day having a family and raising their children in a democracy, where they could work hard and build a small business from her writing, maybe a publishing company, while he would go into politics, local government, and who knew how far the future would take them.

But those were the exciting times, still years away. Right now, they were saddled in the 'dark days,' as they called them, yet the impatience and energy of their struggle made them not feel so dark. Instead, she was invigorated, especially since someone had struck at the MSS.

No one seemed to know what information was taken or what the courier was carrying, but everyone knew that the couriers only trafficked the most highly sensitive data that couldn't be trusted on the networks. Quan had said it might be enough. Enough to spark a full revolution. He told her that the MSS reaction with raids and mass arrests was a sure sign that they were scared.

She was scared too, although she didn't want to admit it to Quan. People she knew had been taken in a round up only an hour earlier. The government seemed to know who was against them.

The door opened, startling her, as it always did, but this time she actually jumped. With instant relief, she saw it was the skinny, tousled hair, dark-eyed guy she adored. Even though he was busy and hyped up with all the action, he still gave her a hug and a kiss before delivering the news to her. She began typing as he animatedly spoke, complete with large arm swings and contorted facial antics, of arrests and rumors. She would be able to upload it all the instant he finished his report.

"The courier has been arrested," he said. "Because although injured, they suspected he had been in on it."

"That's terrible. Could he have been?" Her question had incredible significance, because the MSS vetted their couriers almost more than they did their own agents. Since these men and women generally worked alone, with little supervision, their identities were known to only a few high placed MSS officials. "I mean, if a courier has betrayed the brutal organization, then that must mean one of the other dissident groups has come a long way—found a way in, to turn a top spy."

It was too risky for the different factions and groups to communicate, but there was a vast network of underground information exchanged, which emboldened the students.

"I think so," he answered excitedly. "I'm sorry for the courier, but thrilled for our movement."

She continued typing information as he dictated. There was much to report—protests, planned meetings, disappearances. "We should post this. And then go eat," Ping said. "Because we'll be at the meeting late into the night."

"The MSS is watching for two specific fugitives, not just the crackdowns to stop any further problems. They are devoting lots of resources in seeking those two people."

"Who are they?" she asked, continuing to type.

"I've heard from someone on the train. It was a Chinese woman and an American."

"Could that really be? An American?"

"I hope so, because—"

The door burst open again. This time there were shouts. Orders not to move. And there were guns. Lots of guns.

Chapter Fifty-Five

In the safehouse barracks, Wen was tossing weapons and clothes into a bag when Chase walked in.

He looked around, a seasoned trainee from being around Wen so long, quick eye movements into corners, ceiling, everything scanned in less than a moment. "Are we leaving now?"

"We've found Yǐn Huāshù."

"The children?" Chase asked. "Where? How?"

"The Astronaut orchestrated a miracle, dissected life out of dead data, and came up with a location. Jang House. Angúo is getting us a car. We should be able to be there tonight, and get inside first thing in the morning."

"Are they alive?"

She nodded. "He thinks so."

"And you're on board with this?"

Wen smiled. "The children will lead the way."

Ping and Quan exchanged horrified expressions as six MSS agents quickly filled the cramped space. A tall woman shoved Ping roughly to the floor. Quan, trying to help her, lunged toward them. Two different agents fired. Bullets from both guns tore through his twenty-two year-old body and he fell, instantly dead.

Ping jumped up, screaming in mournful, terror-stricken agony. She kicked and flung her arms, trying to get to his body, but three of them wrestled her back to the floor and cuffed her. She continued yelling and crying until the female agent slapped her hard across the face.

"He's dead, don't waste your breath," the agent hissed. "You're going to end up getting yourself in more trouble if you keep—"

Ping spit in her face.

"Or get yourself killed," the woman said, snapping Ping's neck in a blurred motion. She reached down and took the cuffs off Ping's crumpled body. "There, now you're with your boyfriend again." She walked out.

Chase and Wen were driving into the setting sun when Tess called. "You can't go to BioCheng tonight," the CISS director said, as if it were her permission to grant.

"Why?" Chase asked. He and Wen had already decided to go to the hidden flowers first, since the children could be moved or killed at any moment. "Shen Hán not working out?"

"It's not him. We've analyzed recent MSS movements and intercepted certain information. They are anticipating an attack on either BioCheng or the other lab where he was heading."

"You know what happened to the courier?" Wen asked.

"He's in prison, recovering from his injuries."

Wen's face fell, knowing the man would likely be tortured and then executed. *I should have killed him.* In a perfect world, she would get together a team and break him out of prison, but that was not possible. Another death on her.

"We're running out of time," Chase said to Tess. "We need to get out of the country tomorrow, but first we need to get to the lab."

"Don't go tonight, unless you want to join the courier."

Chase decided not to tell her about the children. "What are you seeing with the MSS about us? How close are they?"

"Nice move on the plane," Tess said. "They don't know where you are, but they're arresting so many people they could stumble into you without even realizing it. Keep your head down, and wait until we get a go-ahead from Shen Hán."

"We're leaving China tomorrow," Chase said firmly.

"I'll be back in touch."

Wen removed the SIM card from the phone. "Why are we letting her dictate what we do?"

"We weren't going tonight anyway," Chase said. "And we need her help."

"Do we?"

"You're good, but are you good enough to get into a secure facility when they're expecting us?"

"We didn't need Tess to tell us the MSS is waiting for us. We've lit up the entire country." Wen checked the side mirror. "I can get in. We can do it."

"You'll have that chance tomorrow night."

She glared at him.

"You're upset about the courier," he said, taking her hand. She shook him off.

"Yes, I am. But that is not why. This operation does not have anything to do with Tess."

"Is it because she's CIA? And you're still conditioned, from all your years of training, to consider them the enemy?"

"They *are* the enemy."

"And so is the MSS, and the Russian intelligence, and the Mossad, and all of them, but this is about China. We risked our lives to come here again."

"So many people have already died that would still be alive had we not come back."

"It's up to us."

"I would not have come if it was just about China."

"This is about all of us. Our future."

She looked out the window, quiet and moody, fighting to keep focused and not sink into despair. The sky melted magenta with streaks of orange. She loved China, and its people, but hated what it had become under the communist dictatorship.

Chase knew she was carrying far more weight than him. He had come on another quest to save humanity, but she had come for different reasons—for China, for the MSS, for her sister, for her father, and for unfinished stories.

Chapter Fifty-Six

The man who had to wake Minister Li wished he could be somewhere else. The Minister did not like to be woken, and he also did not like the news.

"*What?*" Li barked, as if he hadn't been asleep at all.

The MSS agent identified himself. "Sir, there is an issue. It just came in. We've been monitoring Dr. Tián's communications at BioCheng."

"Yes, I ordered it. What do you have?"

"It seems Dr. Tián has not been entirely truthful."

"About what?" Li asked impatiently, wondering if he would be able to get back to sleep.

"The children."

"What children?" Li asked, now knowing there would be no sleep.

"The test subjects."

"They are dead . . . their records destroyed," Li said, wishing he wasn't about to hear what he was about to hear.

"Apparently not, sir."

"The children are *alive?*"

"Yes."

"Where?"

While the agent was telling Li the location of the children, and other details they had discovered, including the fact that Dr. Tián had been following the progress of the children for years after their supposed termination, Li was seeing his life flash before his eyes.

"We have to get there before . . . " Li said as he jumped out of bed and began dressing.

"Before what?"

"Malone and the woman!"

The facility looked more like a nursing home back in America, or a senior center for assisted living. The grounds were manicured, with an abundance of trees—a pretty campus nestled and hidden in a rural setting. Nothing anyone would easily notice from the air. Chase and Wen had traveled several miles down a private road, without signs or markers, just off the highway to find it.

"This place is designed to attract no attention," Chase said. "Nothing around for miles."

"But there are no children playing," Wen said. "If there were children here, wouldn't they be playing outside?"

"Perhaps, but maybe they're doing school now," Chase said, looking at the facility again, wondering if his optimistic explanation was naïve. There was no playground equipment visible, no loose toys, nothing even colorful that young children would like.

Wen watched the trees and the windows, wondering if a surprise was coming. She was happy that they weren't having to take the building by force, or even to sneak in.

The odds would have been too great that the children could have been injured or killed. The thought made her shiver.

However, that would not be necessary. Through an incredible stroke of luck, they were actually invited guests. Mei Lein had worked the networks of dissidents as soon as Wen told her where they were going. It turned out that someone knew someone who knew the head mistress of Jang House, and she was sympathetic. She'd been told that government officials were considering closing the facility and the fate of the children was at risk. Chase and Wen were there to document what had happened.

They walked to the main entrance and found it locked. Wen looked into the camera. Chase wondered what face they would see since they were both wearing a fresh application of vIDs. A buzzer soon let them inside, where the sight that greeted them was more along the lines of a hospital than a nursing home.

"Everything is so sterile," Wen whispered, as a petite, gray-haired Chinese woman walked down the hall toward them. She gave them a nervous smile.

"Good morning. My name is Suyin."

Chase and Wen introduced themselves, using aliases.

"I don't want to get any trouble," she said. "I am doing this to protect the children."

Wen assured her that they would make sure she was not to blame. Suyin spoke rapid Chinese to Wen that Chase would later learn was a series of questions about if they had been followed, or if anyone knew they were coming. She looked several times at the hall's camera.

"You are very brave," Wen told her, knowing that being caught having even a conversation with her and Chase would have meant the death penalty. Wen gave Suyin many assurances until she finally agreed to take them to meet the children.

Suyin spoke a little English. "The children in school now."

Chase looked at Wen and smiled. He had been right.

"It's not like normal school. These are not normal children."

At the end of the long hall, she stopped at a keypad and tapped in what Chase noted was a sixteen digit code of which he only got seven.

Another hall. Many doors, before Suyin finally opened one.

Chase almost gasped at the sight on the other side—six little girls, all in matching gray and white uniforms. He estimated their ages to be between three and six years old. "Yǐn Huāshù," he said softly to himself.

"Are these all the children?" Wen asked.

Suyin shook her head, then walked over to a locked filing cabinet, punched in a code that Chase didn't see, and opened a drawer. She handed Wen a stack of folders. While Chase surveyed the room, Wen leafed through the folders, all written in Chinese, of course. Chase smiled at the little girls, who were sneaking peaks at him. None of them returned the smile except one, perhaps the oldest. Her eyes lit up as if she'd just been given a gift.

"Each of these girls has had genes edited as embryos. Yǐn Huāshù are real," Wen whispered to Chase.

He smiled, but at the same time felt queasy, looking at the pretty faces of the innocent young girls who had no idea what had been done to them before their birth, and, judging by this facility, had also been robbed of a normal childhood. "Will she let you take the files?"

Wen asked Suyin in Mandarin.

Suyin shook her head "You take digital copies of the most important pages."

He continued to smile at the girls and even gave a slight wave. None waved back. Yet he noticed the same bright-eyed girl raise her pinky and ring finger slightly off her desk, twice, as if considering waving back.

Chapter Fifty-Seven

After visiting a second room, also containing only girls, Suyin took Chase and Wen to a third door, where, once again, she entered a long series of numbers on the keypad. Chase got nine of them before the door opened.

"It's a boy," Chase said, surprised.

"Yes," Suyin said. "Tu is the only male subject at Jang House."

"How old is he?" Chase asked, noting that he appeared to be the eldest of the children.

"Tu, tell these people how old you are," Suyin said in Mandarin.

The little boy seemed shy, yet at the same time curious and excited to see visitors, particularly Chase. He held up seven fingers. Chase was amazed it had been going on that long. He smiled at Tu and held up ten fingers closed his fist, and repeated it until he had showed the boy that he was thirty.

Tu said a long sentence in Mandarin and shook his head.

"What did he say?" Chase asked, turning to Wen.

Tu answered in English before Wen could. "I said that you are too old to be counting with your fingers. Not as old as Suyin is, but you are still very, very old."

Chase laughed. "You speak better English than I do."

"I have never been to England," Tu said. "Is that where you are from?"

"No, I'm from America."

The boy's eyes widened. "America? Is it real?"

Chase thought the boy was joking, and almost laughed again, but quickly saw he was quite sincere in his question.

"Yes, America is real. It's a big and exciting place."

Tu looked at him for a moment, as if deciding whether or not to believe him. "I thought America was just in stories," he said, looking puzzled. "A make-believe place."

"It is definitely real," Chase assured him, then looked at Wen, hoping she would corroborate his claim.

"It is a wonderful place," Wen said to him in Mandarin. "I have been there. You would like it."

"I would?" Tu smiled. "Can we go there?"

Suyin shook her head. "No, no. But maybe they will tell you a story about America."

Tu looked disappointed. "One day, I would like to visit this place, America. But I have never even left Jang House."

Chase and Wen exchanged a sad glance.

"Do you speak any other languages?" Wen asked.

"Yes, I speak Spanish," he replied in Spanish. "And French," he said in French. "And Japanese, and Korean, and German, and Italian, and my favorite, Swahili." Each response was spoken in a different language.

Chase didn't have to guess which genes had been manipulated in Tu. Clearly they had been going for high intelligence. It made sense it would be the first place they would start.

"Tu, if I asked you what the square root of seventeen-hundred-twenty-nine was? Could you answer that?"

"Yes, it is easy," Tu said. "41.581245772584."

"He and the Astronaut would get along quite well," Wen said.

"An astronaut? Do you know an astronaut?" Tu asked, and then began naming Chinese, US, and Soviet Astronauts, reciting space trivia, space facts, and listing various rocket types before Chase interrupted him.

"Not that kind of an astronaut, I'm afraid," Chase said. "It's only something we call him because he is very smart, like you."

"I would like to meet him. Is he in America?"

"No, he's in Europe right now."

"Could we go there, then? I can speak all the languages, and I know all the cities. I could tell you their populations and the leader of each country."

"Not now," Suyin said.

Tu looked disappointed again. "I know all these things, but I don't get to talk with other people about these things. So all these things just stay in my head for no reason, and I would like to be able to use them." He looked imploringly at Wen.

"Maybe we can arrange a phone call with the Astronaut sometime for you," Wen said, then looked at Suyin, whose face revealed she thought the idea was absolutely horrible.

Tu was staring at Chase now. "Do you have another question, Tu?" Chase asked.

"Can I touch your skin?" he asked. "I have never seen pale skin like yours in real life. Does it feel like mine? It looks like it would be very cold."

Chase held out his arm. Tu touched his skin, softly at first, and then squeezed, and finally pinched it lightly, as if trying to pull it off.

"Ouch," Chase said playfully.

Tu pulled his fingers away quickly. "I'm sorry. I'm so sorry Mr. American."

Chase smiled and gave an easy laugh. "No, I was only teasing. It didn't hurt."

"Oh." Tu looked unsure.

"Really," Chase said. "It's okay."

"We should go," Suyin said. "To finish copying the records."

Wen nodded.

Chase squatted down next to the boy. "Tu, I have really enjoyed talking to you. And I very much hope we will meet again." He held out his hand to shake.

Tu seemed too nervous to shake hands. Instead, he bowed slightly. "I would like that also, Mr. American."

"Chase. Please call me Chase."

"Okay, like JP Morgan Chase Bank, sixth largest in the world by assets, two-point-six-trillion dollars. Is JP Morgan Chase *your* bank?"

"No, just the same name."

"Okay, it's not the biggest bank anyway. The world's biggest bank is in China—Industrial and Commercial Bank of China, four-point-one-trillion dollars in assets. In fact, the top four largest banks in the world are Chinese, with more than fifteen-trillion."

Chase reluctantly waved goodbye. Tu snapped his fingers twice and then saluted.

As soon as Chase and Wen were back in the hallway with Suyin, Chase whispered to Wen, "We have to take Tu with us."

Chapter Fifty-Eight

After she had scanned all of the critical documents onto her micro-drive, Wen looked at Suyin. "We would like to take Tu with us."

Suyin's eyes filled with shock, as if she'd just been told some horrible news. She shook her head. "No, that cannot be possible."

"This is no life for him here," Wen said. "Please, do not be offended, but he cannot grow here. He is a laboratory sample."

"The scientists, they will be here for inspections. They will have us arrested."

"The authorities will come, and the children will tell them we were here," Wen said. "Risk is very big to leave him here, plus there is *no future* for him."

"We'll take out the cameras," Chase said. "Make it like we broke in and took the children by force."

"No, no," Suyin repeated. "This is too dangerous. I should never let you in."

"It's too late," Wen said.

Suyin knew the damage had been done, and part of her, if she could have been honest and not afraid, would have admitted that she was glad they were taking Tu. He was too special, and needed something more. Still, she was terrified. Suyin had always tried to do the right thing, to help other people, and now, for the first time in her life, she feared for it. Prison or death—awful choices.

"What will you do with him?"

"Get him out of the country and make sure he has a good life," Wen said, knowing Suyin could not say no. Tu was the living proof of what the Chinese scientists had done. "They won't let him live."

"You think it is hard to move through China without getting captured, doing it with a boy will be much harder—especially a boy who has never been in the outside world."

The two women looked deeply into each other's eyes, instinctively knowing, in these moments, that they shared many similarities and strengths. They also understood it was possible both might die, and yet each realized that what they were doing, in opposition to their homeland, justified whatever sacrifice had to be made.

As the two turned away, each felt, with complete certainty, they would never see each other again in this lifetime.

"You should ask Tu if he wants to go," Chase said.

"He doesn't really have a choice," Wen replied.

"He will want to go."

The three of them headed back to Tu's room.

"Chase Bank, you are back very quickly," Tu said when he saw them come in. Chase looked around at Tu's room, which seemed barely better than a prison cell—white tiled walls, gray tiled floor, a fluorescent lamp, a tiny window. No toys, no color. A standard uniform and towel.

"Would you like to come with us?" Chase asked.

"Come with you to eat?"

"No, to go to live somewhere else."

"To live in America?"

"Maybe," Chase said, smiling. "Somewhere that isn't here. Somewhere happier."

Tu looked at Suyin. She nodded slightly.

"I would like to go try this," Tu said.

Chase and Wen glanced at each other, trying to decide whether they should tell him he would never be coming back, or to trust in the fact that once he was out of there, he never would want to return. There didn't seem to be any easy answer.

"Okay," Chase said. "We'll try it."

"I'll help you get ready," Suyin told him.

Chase's phone vibrated.

"It's from Tess," he said to Wen, as he started to read the secure text.

They know it's you, and they know where you are. Get out now!

Chapter Fifty-Nine

The Astronaut called a minute later. "The MSS is on the way. They have orders to terminate the program. That means everything will be destroyed . . . including the children."

Wen quickly explained to Suyin what had happened while Chase destroyed the cameras and the server that stored their data.

Suyin and another staff member rounded up the girls. The plan was if they got caught, they would say they were fleeing in order to prevent Chase and Wen from taking all the children.

"Where are they going?" Tu asked, looking out the car window as the girls were getting into two cars.

"Field trip," Chase said. "Wouldn't be fair if you get to leave and they don't get to go anywhere."

"Where to?"

"A dairy farm," Chase said, unsure why that answer popped into his head.

He made a disgusted face. "We'll have more fun,

won't we?"

"You bet!"

Li took a call from the official in charge of the region where Jang House was located. "We arrived about seven minutes ago," he reported. "The children are gone."

The Minister suddenly felt as if he were taking punches in a boxing ring. "How long ago?"

"The place was abandoned, but one of our people found a staff member walking home. She told us that two people showed up, and they are described as—"

"An American man with a Chinese woman," Li interrupted.

"Yes, that's right," the official said, surprised, but not really too surprised, knowing Li's reputation. "They have quite a head start. More than an hour."

"You find them. You *find* them."

"We'll put everyone on it."

"I have several teams on the way."

"If we get them before your people arrive, what are our orders?"

"Kill the children. But I want that couple alive."

"Yes, sir," the official said, sounding a little reluctant.

"There is no greater priority than to find them. Everything is second to that—your career, your life, they are not as important to the Party. Understand?"

"Of course."

Li hung up. He called key people to throw extra resources into finding Chase Malone and the woman while bringing up all the zones close to the Jang House on the monitors in his office. He had miscalculated, thinking they were going to one of the labs, but instead they had gone for the children—the children he'd recommended killing years before. Instead, others would now die for allowing them to live. He'd already ordered the arrest of Dr. Tián.

Shen arrived a few minutes later to happily confirm that indeed, Dr. Tián was in custody. Although a trial might occur at some date in the future, no doubt remained that the doctor would be executed. However, the first priority was to make sure they knew everything that Tián knew.

"Have you told the president?" Shen asked.

Li looked at him as if it were a silly question, but he answered it anyway. "If I tell the president, he will ask me to resign."

Shen looked at him, realizing he was right, but only nodded.

"We must find those damned children. If Malone gets out of China with them, we will not be able to deny Mìng Rénshēng."

Shen thought about it, wondering what the ramifications of that might be. *Would the party shut the program down? War with whoever this couple was working for? Continue the Mìng Rénshēng anyway? Why would they take the kids? Surely they didn't need them for the data, they could get all that from the labs. The minister is right, they took the children for proof. They are trying to end China's program, and that realization changes things.*

"They have proved elusive thus far," Shen began. "What if we don't catch them?"

"Then you might just get your wish. Mìng Rénshēng will be terminated, and so will I."

He stared at Shen and held his gaze. The two men knew the stakes. It was unlikely Shen would survive such a traumatic shakeup either. He was technically not the number two man in the MSS, but by being so close to Li, he had assumed an unofficial deputy position. Shen had enemies and rivals within the MSS himself. They absolutely must find Malone and the woman, and getting the kids was equally crucial.

"This is not the way I want the program to end," Shen said, never taking his eyes away from Li's.

The minister believed his lieutenant not because their trust and loyalty were unwavering, but because logic said it was the best way.

Chapter Sixty

Li could feel it slipping away. Malone now had the Mìng Rénshēng children. *How has one couple done so much damage in so short a time?* Li wondered as he ordered heightened border security in anticipation of Chase and the woman fleeing the country with the children.

Li had made a call to the president. He hadn't wanted to tell him about the children, but knew China well enough to know that the president would eventually be told by someone, and he had better hear it first from his Minister of State Security. The president listened carefully before responding.

"I understand you were deceived about the children, yet in your job, deception can only belong to you. Understand?"

"Yes."

"Li, I'm afraid the only thing that can save you now is the apprehension and execution of the fugitives and all the remaining Mìng Rénshēng children."

After the call, Li ordered an intensification of the crackdown. "It's time to destroy the resistance," he told a subordinate, and then thought bitterly, *If I go down, by hell, there will be no dissident left standing.*

Mars got word to Chase via the Astronaut that he had finally cracked the surveillance system in China.

"Starting now," Chase told Wen, "you and I are about to be in twenty places at once."

"Mars is a genius," Wen said. "He's going to save our lives."

"Mars is the fourth planet from the sun," Tu said. "Approximately 227,940,000 kilometers from our little yellow dwarf star. Mars is named for the Roman god of war. It has the tallest mountain in our solar system—Olympus Mons is twenty-one kilometers high. It's actually a shield volcano that was formed billions of years ago."

"Not that Mars," Chase said.

"Oh," Tu said, confused. "There's another one?"

Chase and Wen found her grandmother, bent over, working in an expansive garden. Zǔ mǔ turned around, having seen their shadows come across a row of onions. She had the grainy look of a woman who had lived a hard life.

Her expression filled with astonishment, adoration, and unfallen tears at the sight of Wen. She got to her feet and walked slowly toward Wen, as if savoring each step, steps that contained memories and feelings she never thought would be real again.

"Oh, Wen Sung, you've come home. It is really you?"

She took in the scene of Chase and Tu, and then wrapped her arms around Wen, holding her with trembling strength that made clear her intense love for her granddaughter. Chase knew Wen was her only living descendent, but he wasn't sure if Zǔ mǔ had believed, up to that moment, that Wen was dead.

The rapid exchange of words in Mandarin could only be understood by them. By Tu's expression, Chase could tell that the speed and shorthand between the two women was even more than his highly evolved mind could translate. Zǔ mǔ quickly got the story, because Chase watched her face go from elation, to concern, to fear, to anger. The animated woman had a history of modern China etched on her face. He could see where Wen got her strength and determination. In spite of the fear in her eyes, Chase believed Zǔ mǔ to be a fearless woman. One capable of as much as Wen was in a different arena. She knew the old ways, a power more fierce than the MSS because of its anchor in tradition, family, and rightness.

Zǔ mǔ knelt down and looked Tu in the eyes and spoke softly to him. Chase didn't know what she was saying, but it sounded like an old wizard telling a story of magic, shamans, castles, and knights. Chase watched as Tu's eyes responded in wonderment, as if he was falling in love with the old woman as she spoke, and he knew it would be okay to leave Tu with her. Even with that thought, he couldn't help but look up into the sky and wonder if the MSS knew where they were.

Wen explained that they could not stay long. "I'm sorry, but we need you to look after the boy while we go and take care of something."

Zǔ mǔ looked at Wen, as if asking her many questions. Wen replied to perhaps the most dire of the unspoken ones.

"If we don't come back, it means we are dead."

"Like your father." Zǔ mǔ shook her head. "You think you can change the world, that you can save the world. The world is big. There are smaller worlds, worlds where you could be safe, happy. Worlds like this." She waved her arm out over the trees, toward a reflection of the lake in the distance, visible through a break in the leaves.

"Someday, I would like to be in a smaller world," Wen said. "But these beautiful worlds are only possible if the bigger one is balanced."

Zǔ mǔ nodded. After all, she had taught Wen all about balance.

"If we don't come back, will you take care of Tu?"

"Of course."

"He is special."

"I can see that."

"They made him that way."

Zǔ mǔ gave her a concerned and sad expression.

"He doesn't know."

"It is okay, Wen. He and I will be fine. And you will come back."

Chapter Sixty-One

Minister Li stood in the command center part of the MSS complex and barked orders to subordinates. "Where is Shen? He should have been here by now."

"I believe he's only a few minutes away," somebody said.

"Sir, we've got another Chase Malone sighting. This time in Beijing."

"Follow it," Li said, annoyed that in the past three hours there had been more than a hundred alerts that Chase Malone had been seen by surveillance cameras all across China, Hong Kong, and several other areas of the world that the MSS monitored.

"Sir, obviously they have hacked our system," a tall, skinny man wearing eyeglasses said. "Malone must be trying to throw us off. He may be trying to make us think he's after something other than what he really wants."

"Exactly," Li said impatiently. "Which is precisely why one of these sightings is real, or the next one might be. We can't afford to ignore them."

"That's just what he wants. That, and spreading our

resources too thin. We're already at the breaking point in some regions."

Li nodded. He knew all of this. Malone was a smart man, and the minister had come to believe that he and Malone weren't both going to survive the next twenty-four hours.

Li stared at the list of sightings on the big screen, all strategically important locations—dozens within a few miles of every lab in the program, but there were also sightings near major tech companies, including most of the ones involved in spying, military technologies, and Sky Net surveillance firms. "Malone could be using the whole program as a false flag. Perhaps Mìng Rénshēng is not what he's interested in at all," Li told an analyst focusing solely on how Chase was continually able to avoid detection. They had a sense of what vIDs was now, but still had no idea how it worked.

"Mìng Rénshēng isn't Malone's area," the analyst, who had studied the American billionaire during the last four hours, said. "However, military technology, other artificial intelligence, and machine learning are."

Li felt a sense of panic, an unnatural emotion for him. He wasn't entirely sure what Chase Malone was up to, but what if it *wasn't* Mìng Rénshēng? Identifying the woman might help.

The Minister called a general and requested troops to be sent to all the labs in the Mìng Rénshēng program, and additional troops sent to any facility that had anything to do with artificial intelligence, machine learning, or advanced military technologies. Another analyst had prepared a list of them, which was forwarded to the general.

The timid man from earlier reappeared in the command center and told Li what he already knew.

"There is one hundred percent certainty that the man you are looking for is Chase Malone." The man explained how this had been verified, and quickly showed Li a presentation on his laptop of the different places Malone had been since he had entered the country.

"Can you extrapolate from that where he is now?" Li asked.

The timid man nodded hesitantly.

"Not in twelve hours," Li said firmly. "I need to know in the next twelve minutes. Find a place to work. Do it now." Li walked away without giving the man a chance to say no.

Li had also summoned the other two "experts", who had been trying to identify Wen. They reported to the command center, armed with diagrams and charts. "The MSS database was definitely hacked," one of them said. "It was such a precision operation that everything associated with one agent was removed and nothing else."

"Every single reference to her that may have appeared in any other agent or officer's files was also removed," the other one continued. "It is impossible to trace. It was a brilliant strike, and went undetected because it was so small."

"Have you interviewed all the commanders?" Li asked. "Someone must remember her and know who she was."

"We have begun the process, but there are many dead. We did, however, tag three of the deceased for further study —Xiang, Ling, and Lo. They cannot be interviewed."

"Rong Lo?" Li asked, remembering the case. "He was our best. We lost him in America. That's the one. Concentrate on his people."

"Okay, but still . . . it will be time consuming," the first man said, as they all heard two more Chase Malone alerts come in.

"I don't care if we have to interview every single person

in MSS. I want a full investigation. We must piece this together manually and find out who she was. Who she *is*."

"Do we have that time?" the man pressed. "It could take a year."

Li glared at him. "Then you better start now."

The Minister looked around the command center, knowing that somebody in there might know who she is, could have even helped her. He didn't trust anyone, but he knew, with certainty, that it had been Chase Malone that must have pulled off the hack that had erased her identity.

What else might he have done?

Li gave the order to kill them both and rescinded his earlier order to take them alive. "Kill them without regard to civilian safety or casualties, and kill everyone around them—especially children!"

Chapter Sixty-Two

Tess looked at the screen in mission control, wondering how long Chase and Wen could continue to avoid detection.

"You're leaving a trail of bodies in China," the CISS director said. "The Communist Party frowns on others doing that rather than themselves."

Chase, impatient, already knowing the dangerous spot they were in, responded gruffly, "Do you have any information that can help us, or not?"

Normally Tess would've snapped back, but she didn't want their last conversation to be a typical war of words. "We've heard from the lieutenant. BioCheng is virtually impossible to penetrate. It's a building within a building. The exterior walls are twenty-four inches thick. Every surveillance imaginable."

"But there is a flaw, right?"

"Shen Hán does have an idea. If we can get the power shut down, you might have a chance."

"I assume there's a backup generator?"

"Of course. You would have to take that out as well.

Then the facility will automatically lock down in the event of a complete power failure."

"I'm sure you have an answer for that as well."

"There would never be time to get through walls that thick. However, the roof is a composite concrete that's only ten inches thick."

"That's still a lot to go through. We'd need diamond blades and portable saws, and even then it will take—"

"Close to twenty minutes, according to our experts."

"The blades could be tough to get, and even with lubrication cooling, we'll need at least—"

"With dulling and wear, it should take six of them to get through depending on the diamond coating and surface. Once inside, you'll require a special drill to remove the secure hard drive, which is a little over two feet long by eight inches wide."

"And while we're doing this, the MSS will be on the way," Wen said.

"Yes," Tess said. "You'll have to get in and back out of the roof in twenty-nine minutes."

"That's too long," Wen said. "The MSS would take less than half of that time to respond. And local police could be there in five minutes."

"We have some ways of slowing both response times."

"How?"

"Classified."

"Un-classify it," Wen said. "I don't like counting on invisible things to help."

"Too bad," Tess said. "You're going to have to."

"Is there another way in?" Chase asked. "Can't lieutenant Shen just open the doors for us?"

"No."

"Can you help us source any of the materials?" Chase asked.

"I'll see what we can do, but you're in China. It's all readily available." She gave them some additional instructions, then ended the call.

"It's a death trap," Wen said to Chase, as she called WOLF. "We won't make it out of there alive, and Tess doesn't care."

Chase didn't answer, but handed Wen a list of what they needed.

Mei Lein told Wen they could have everything within two hours. Chase and Wen would need every minute of that time to plan their attack.

"Nice to hear you are continuing to defy the odds," the Astronaut said upon hearing Wen's voice.

"It's especially good for us, too," Wen said. "We need a favor."

"Another one? That seems to be a regular thing."

"Can you take down the power grid?" She gave him the coordinates.

"Anywhere else in the world, I would say yes, but as you know, everything is different in China. They use a Clyme-3900 security encryption, with extra ramification-autonomy to protect their grid."

"I'm glad you're familiar with it then. Can you do it?"

"It is definitely possible, but I would need a few days. How long before you need it?"

"A few hours."

"Of course you do."

"It's critical. If we can get that done, we can grab the

drive and be in and out of BioCheng. Then we can leave China."

"I'll figure out a way," the Astronaut said, as if it were a routine request he was fulfilling.

Angúo and a female WOLF operative, Jo Shei, showed up in a van, carrying the materials. After introductions, Angúo told them that there was a car parked waiting for them half a block away.

"Great," Chase said. "Hope we need it."

"Unfortunately, we could only get five blades," Jo said. "Very sorry. It was extremely difficult to get these on such short notice. They are industrial grade, not available through regular stores."

"We'll just have to make them work."

"If they don't," Jo said, holding up a sledgehammer, "we've got this."

In the moonless night, they parked near the BioCheng facility and waited. The Astronaut was going to knock the power out for three square miles. Tess could not do it because the Chinese would see CIA "fingerprints" on the operation.

"Why isn't it down yet?" Chase asked impatiently as the time frame the Astronaut had given passed.

"He'll get it," Wen said. "It's not like it's easy to remotely take out power in a major Chinese city."

"It should've gone dark by now," Jo said.

"He could be running into an issue," Wen said.

"Yeah, like it's impossible," Chase said.

"He's never let us down before."

The four of them, all dressed in black, reviewed the plan again. As soon as the grid went dark, they would take out the exterior guards, blow the generator, and then start cutting into the roof.

Suddenly, they were in a sea of absolute darkness, except for BioCheng, which remain illuminated, although muted.

"He did it!" Chase said.

"We've got another problem," Wen said, and they all instantly saw what she had seen—a troop carrier with more than a dozen PLA soldiers heading straight for them.

Chapter Sixty-Three

The troop-carrier pulled to a stop twenty-five feet in front of them. The soldiers stood up and started exiting the open back of the vehicle. A second truck squealed in behind them. Even before Wen, Chase, and the two WOLF operatives could get out of their van, the other trucks and all the troops were drowned in an electric blue light.

"What the hell is that?" Chase asked as the soldiers all collapsed, presumably dead.

"That is Tess," Wen said, certain it could only be the United States, and happy she'd been wrong about Tess—at least for today.

"Tess?"

"That's an advanced space-based weapon system."

"How do you know?" Chase asked as they jumped out of the van.

"Because I've never seen anything like that," Wen replied, her voice full of awe.

They all stood stunned and silent, looking at the motionless soldiers.

"We have to keep moving," Wen whispered, not aware she'd said anything.

The blue light disappeared. Chase and Jo ran to the outer wall and began preparing explosives to blow their way in. Angúo started unloading materials while Wen went to clear the area.

Wen ran silently into the darkness and found the guards by sound. She emerged from the shadows near the dimly lit building amid the distant hum of the generator. The armed man, clearly alarmed by the city-wide blackout, had apparently not seen the "alien attack" on the PLA truck. Wen hoped to merely render the man unconscious, but small stray lights crossed over her at the last instant and illuminated her approach. This gave the guard time to react, and meant Wen had no choice but to use lethal force.

The unexpected light had come from another guard, who had deviated from his normal rounds, apparently due to the power outage. He spotted Wen just as she snapped the neck of the first man. The guard swung his gun around and pointed his weapon.

Spinning and ducking at the same time, Wen knew the second guard had her. She'd been in too many similar situations. There was no way she could get her gun aimed and fired before his bullet reached her. Her mind burned with the imprints from hundreds of fights while her eyes searched the murky darkness for any advantage. Everything told her she was about to die.

Chase and Jo took cover, counted, checked the area, and then detonated the charge. They quickly entered the void in the outer wall, and among the rubble, planted the next round of explosives, designed to disable the generator. Its protections were numerous—the main target was two large propane tanks which fueled the power source of last resort.

They set the timer and ran back to the staging area, where Angúo had already unloaded the rest of the gear.

Only the sound of the explosion saved Wen's life. The generator's propane tanks erupted in a thunderous booming noise, sending a fire ball high above the building. The timing of the blast that she knew was coming could not have been better.

The guard lost focus, his hand shook, and the shot went wide. By the time he recovered, she had slipped into the darkness. He shone a spotlight in sweeps around where she'd been, but caught nothing. With his gun held next to the light, and leading the way, the guard moved hesitantly toward his fallen partner. A second later, he was dead.

Chase and Jo brought the extension ladder, saw, blades, and drill to the back of the main lab building. Amidst the smoke and flames, they climbed onto the roof and hoisted up the heavy saw.

At the same time, on the other side of the building, Wen was searching for three more guards they had been told would be patrolling outside. She found two of them taking Angúo into custody.

Chapter Sixty-Four

They had not calculated the destructive power of the full propane tanks. One end of the building was in flames, which brought another threat, as firefighters would likely respond before they could complete their mission. Chase, using the GPS coordinates that Tess had provided, began sawing. Prior to the blue light annihilation of the troops, Chase had worried that CISS might not be able to pinpoint exactly where they should cut into the roof. However, after watching all those soldiers drop at the same time, he was a believer.

The plan was to cut four sides and angles roughly eighteen inches each. He and Jo took turns operating the big saw and checking the perimeter of the roof, watching for more MSS, police, firefighters, or any stray lab personnel. They had no idea of the security protocols in place or who would respond after a complete power failure. By now, Angúo should have taken out the phone land lines, and hopefully the Astronaut had done some remote work on the nearest cell towers.

The saw vibrated recklessly. Every four minutes, when they put on a new blade, they traded operations. If it had been straight concrete, the blades wore quickly in the composite concrete, which made the cutting surface much hotter. Jo secured a narrow flexible steel cable ladder, which would be dropped into the opening after they cut through, but only if the blades lasted long enough

---

Tess, in Mission Control, watched firetrucks scramble and head to BioCheng. Gatewood's face loomed large on one of the monitors as he also observed from an undisclosed remote location. Skyenor paced not far from where Tess was seated.

"Gentlemen, those firetrucks cannot be allowed to make it to the lab," Tess said.

"You don't want us to fry a bunch of innocent firefighters, do you?" Skyenor asked.

"Not if we don't have to," Tess replied coolly.

"There's a choke point," Gatewood said, zooming in on a satellite photo of the nearby streets. "I can erase that."

"Taking out the road is risky," Tess said. "How is that going to be explained?"

"It'll look like someone blew it up."

"Not upon close inspection," Tess said. "It'll look melted."

"What about the bridge?" Skyenor asked.

Tess and Gatewood looked farther along on the map.

"Too close to BioCheng," Gatewood said.

"Do it," Tess said.

"It's *too close*," Gatewood repeated.

"We've already taken the cameras out in that quadrant," Tess said.

"What about eyewitnesses at the facility?"

"Wen is running around in the dark," Tess said. "There aren't going to be any witnesses left."

Angúo remained tense, knowing Wen would strike at any minute. He recalled having already been saved by Wen's sister, and felt shame that he required another rescue from a Sung woman. He struggled with the nylon tie that held his wrists locked together and looked for any way to escape.

Wen flew off a ledge near the entrance and killed one of the guards on impact. She rolled and used her victim's body as a shield as the second guard fired. In the maneuver, she managed to get the dead guard's gun and killed the other one.

"Sorry," Angúo said as she cut his bonds.

"For what?"

"Getting caught."

"Forget it. Let's go. There's one more here somewhere."

Two guards suddenly grabbed Wen, dropping a "fox trap" over her head. She knew the device well—an MSS invention of a titanium band which auto-tightened around a subject's torso and arms, effectively making them immobile. She quickly realized they weren't average security guards.

They're MSS, and they knew we'd be here. They were waiting for us. It's a trap, she thought, and then feared Chase might already have been killed or captured.

Chase put in the fifth and final blade roughly seventeen minutes after they started and quietly hoped it would last long enough to get through. They lost almost thirty seconds each time a blade was swapped.

Jo ran to the roof's edge and looked over, trying to find Wen. Instead, she was met with the hands of two MSS agents. Jo, an expert in martial arts, got off a devastating round kick, sending one of them falling backwards, landing on the hard asphalt below. If there had been enough light, Jo could have seen the pool of blood, but she was already wrestling with the second agent, also an expert in martial arts, who had barely made it safely onto the roof and hadn't been able to get to his gun. Chase, wearing ear protection and still cutting, didn't hear the scuffle.

Jo and the agent, exchanging blows, rolled close to the side. The agent, who outweighed her by at least forty pounds, lunged, trying to get a better position, and fired. Jo had anticipated the move and threw all her muscle and weight back at him, even as the bullet ripped into her chest. The two of them sailed off the roof together. Jo rode the agent down as they plunged nearly thirty feet to the pavement. He took the impact and died instantly. Miraculously, Jo climbed off the bigger man, spat on him, walked a few feet back toward the ladder, and then collapsed.

Without knowing it, Chase was up top—an unprotected, open target. He couldn't even hear the approaching MSS helicopter.

Chapter Sixty-Five

Minister Li looked at Shen as the buzz of activity inside the MSS Command Center echoed in urgency. "Trap them? How?"

"They went for the kids. That means we know where they are heading next, and the tracking data confirms it," Shen said.

This was news to Li. "Where?"

"Kaifeng," Shen said, knowing it was hundreds of miles from BioCheng. "The university medical center and bio labs are where the children were born. All the work was done there in the secure sections. They need that data. It is the obvious target. And look at the projected paths. Everything leads to Kaifeng."

Li was convinced. They had agents at all the major labs anyway, and soldiers shoring up the most important facilities. "Order a push to Kaifeng," Li said as another analyst walked briskly toward the Minister.

"Sir, a report has just come in that they have found the

missing girls from Jang House. However, a boy is not with them."

"Were the girls with Malone and the woman?"

"Apparently not. We believe they have the boy. Through intense questioning, the woman in charge of Jang House admitted that Malone and the woman took the boy."

"He is the oldest of the subjects," Shen said. "He was the first."

"Send everything we have available to Kaifeng," Li said. "We are going to end this."

Angúo charged the agents, firing full open with his submachine gun.

"*No!*" Wen yelled, knowing he was committing suicide to save her, but her instincts took over even before the last syllable transformed to fury. Angúo's risky attack took out one of the agents, but not before three of his bullets found Angúo. The agent's bright spotlight hit the ground and lit the angry scene as if they were in a Hollywood gangster film.

In the hail of bullets all around her, Wen went low. Her legs, the only weapons available, kicked and twisted until the only agent still standing was caught in the scissoring vise. Using the ground as leverage and her body as a fulcrum, Wen broke the man's leg. His screams were so agonizingly loud that Wen knew any other guards or agents on the grounds would be there in seconds. She flipped back up to her feet and, without hesitation, kicked in the agent's head. Angúo landed a few feet away, having taken more bullets from the second man. He crawled to her as she finished off the agent.

"You are safe," he whispered.

Wen knew it was what her sister had said to Angúo when she saved him. She also knew she would be in custody, heading toward execution, without him.

"You are brave and honorable Angúo. Thank you."

He smiled weakly. "How do we get you out of that?"

"There is a keypad on the back, four digits. Try one-nine-three-seven." She spun around and kneeled next to him.

"No good," he said, after entering the code.

"Try zero-eight-two-eight."

"Not that either," Angúo said, too slowly.

Wen knew she was losing him, and gave him another code. The MSS used eight different ones for the fox traps.

"Zero-one-three-zero."

Click. The titanium bands fell slack. She turned to thank him again, but Angúo was dead.

Gatewood shook his head. This was as directly involved as HITE had ever been in an ongoing covert operation. It made him nervous, his was the most secret of all US agencies. They were using resources "no one" knew about, things that enemies of the United States would hardly imagine could be real. These were dangerous moves, but Tess had convinced him that what Chase and Wen were doing in China was nothing short of saving humanity, and definitely keeping the US from losing the ultimate biotechnology fight to their most threatening adversary.

Gatewood nodded to his deputy, who, in turn, gave the order to a "pilot," wired up to what looked like a futuristic augmented reality video game.

"The pilot is assuming control of the helicopter," Gatewood explained to Tess, who had been holding her breath as the MSS helicopter flew closer to the BioCheng rooftop where Chase was working, oblivious to his imminent death. She suppressed a scream in her throat. The words, "*Hurry up*," caught in the place in which food became lodged and choked most people, but Tess never choked.

The three secretive spy masters studied the screens in front of them like surgeons as the operation progressed with deadly precision. The pilot sitting in the windowless room of a four-story brick building in a DC suburb easily and silently flew the MSS helicopter away from Chase's roof and into the junction tower of nearby high tension power lines. It was a quick and non-spectacular crash. Almost graceful.

No survivors.

Chapter Sixty-Six

Chase stopped the saw when it became clear the blade was not cutting anymore. "We're still not through," he said as he took off his ear protection. Realizing Jo was not there, he kept low and ran to the ladder, shining his light down on the horrific scene below. The cruel choice he faced tore at him —climb down and see if Jo was still alive, or pick up the sledgehammer and get through.

What would Wen do? he asked himself, and, knowing she would tell him to stick to the mission and let her handle the ground war, Chase ran to the hammer. He pounded at the cut-site, unleashing all his fury and rage. Twelve vicious blows later, the composite concrete roof gave in.

Chase dropped the cable ladder down and wedged himself into the jagged opening. With the large drill and drive carrier, he barely managed to squeeze through, but as soon as he hit the floor inside the impenetrable BioCheng vault, he went straight to work on the server. It was the quicker part of the operation, and yet it took almost eight minutes to get all the screws out. Fortunately, he'd brought a crowbar, as the final casing contained some type of blind-security screws he had no bit for. Chase withdrew the drive, slid it into a protective padded case, and then put that inside a black duffel.

Wen was waiting for him on the roof as he emerged from the hole.

"Got it!" he said, and in the dim glow of their flashlights, their eyes met. "Did you see Jo? Is she . . . ?"

"Let's go," Wen said, and he had his answer.

There was only time for a whispered *thank you* as they ran past Jo's body. It wasn't until they reached the car, waiting half a block from BioCheng, that he asked about Angúo while putting the duffel in the back seat.

"Angúo saved my life," she said. "He didn't make it."

Chase found the keys under the seat and started the engine. "I will always honor his memory."

Wen only nodded.

"Minister, look at this," a technician called him over.

Li studied the readouts with an astounded expression. "Does this mean what I think?"

"Yes, sir. The computers analyzed all the data we have so far, and it appears to be an O.W.S."

Shen, who was standing behind Li, realized he might have made the wrong bet. Orbital Weaponry Systems, or "O.W.S.", were effectively banned by Outer Space Treaty and the SALT II. Both treaties addressed the possibility of weapons of mass destruction in space, space to earth attacks, orbital bombardment, and related offensive tactical uses for space. Only one country could have utilized an O.W.S. to take out two troop carriers at BioCheng.

"The United States is behind this?" Shen asked no one and everyone.

"It's too soon to confirm that it was, in fact, an O.W.S.," the technician cautioned.

Before Li could respond, someone handed him a phone. The call, which he expected might be from the president of China, turned out to be from a scientist who was connected to the original experiment that produced the first few children of the Mìng Rénshēng program.

"The boy is carrying live genetic markers that we must continue to study," the scientist said, as if speaking to a waiter. "The boy wasn't left alive for trivial reasons. He can help us beat AI—show us the future of humanity. If he is killed, we will be a decade behind, and we may never catch up."

"What are you asking?" Li asked, annoyed by one hundred things.

"We need him alive. He must be returned."

After the call, Li turned to Shen. "Rescind the kill order on Malone, the woman, and the boy."

"Are you sure?"

Li nodded, knowing that if the CIA was involved, his career might be saved, but China would most likely go to war with the Americans.

Chapter Sixty-Seven

On the overnight drive to her grandmother's home, Wen and Chase agreed they had to leave China with Tu and Zǔ mǔ. Too many people were after them, and people would never stop looking for the boy.

Tu was asleep when they arrived, just after dawn. Zǔ mǔ was clearly relieved to see them return safely.

Wen explained that they needed to leave the country immediately. "All of us. We also want to take you, too. They will figure out who I am, and come for you."

"I'll be fine."

"No, Zǔ mǔ, you won't. And—"

"Can't you hide Tu in China somewhere? He belongs here."

"He will never be safe anywhere in China," Wen said. "He'd never have a normal life, always hiding, on the run. He is essentially tagged."

"Then you take him, but I cannot leave here," Zǔ mǔ said firmly.

"Why not?" Wen asked.

"This is more than our place. This is where our ancestors are."

"They are wherever we are, Zǔ mǔ."

"No," she said, looking out toward the lake with sad, blurry eyes. "When they flooded Shicheng and the surrounding villages, Qiandao Lake swallowed our family tombs. The temple still holds a sacred vessel which carries the ashes of my grandmother, and her mother, and her grandmother's mother, going back almost one hundred generations."

"Why didn't you get them before they flooded it?"

"I was just a little girl, but we were supposed to have had more time. They didn't want to disturb the resting place of our ancestors." She looked back toward the lake again. "There was some debate in the family about what to do, and how to do it."

"They are at rest there," Chase said.

"Only if they stay connected to a living member of the family. We are the last, me and Wen." She looked at Wen with warmth and love. "So you understand. I cannot leave without them."

"They will find you, Zǔ mǔ, and kill you," Wen said.

"Then I will die here with my people."

"No!" Wen said, her voice breaking. "I will not let you."

"Oh, my sweet Wen Sung, you are so much like your father . . . I would like to be with you, but you know I cannot leave."

"What if I go down and get them?" Wen asked.

"Down? How?" she asked, as if this were something crazy.

"I can dive. I have lots of experience."

Chase knew she was an expert Navy Seal-like diver. He and his brother also used to dive a lot. "Me too."

Wen checked her phone. "There's a sightseeing shop where we can rent gear."

Thirty minutes later, they were at the shop, being fitted for wetsuits, tanks, and the rest. The owner of the shop also rented them a small boat, gave them charts, and told them to avoid restricted areas. Twenty minutes after that, they were at a boat launch, and soon were cruising toward the restricted end of the lake, where Zŭ mŭ told them the ruins of the temple were.

"How did this happen?" Chase shouted above the motor as the boat crossed the expansive waters. The lake, more than two hundred-twenty square miles, at the foot of Wu Shi Mountain, was dotted with more than one thousand large islands, with a few thousand smaller ones scattered across it.

"Qiandao Lake was flooded in 1959 for a major dam project and the population was relocated. The city is eighty to one-hundred-forty feet below the surface. Shicheng was a big place, with hundreds of thousands of inhabitants, and more on the outskirts, like my family, who had been here for more than a millennium."

"Wow. It's hard to believe they would destroy that many people's lives for a dam."

"In China, the government does for the greater good, not the individual."

"Will we be able to find it?" Chase yelled, unaware that they were being watched from the shore.

"The man told me that the city is incredibly well preserved, with buildings and roads dating back to the sixteenth century or older," she answered above the outboard roar while searching the area for any sign of trouble. "Shicheng, known as the 'Lion City,' was built during the Eastern Han Dynasty between AD 25–200."

Chase was fascinated, yet nervous. "Okay, but these are ashes. How will they still be intact?"

"They are in a long, stone urn. It will be sealed. Maybe not watertight, but if the container is intact, the ashes will not be harmed by the water." Feeling completely exposed on the wide open lake, Wen looked toward the sky. "Only a small handful for each family member. The rest were spread to the winds. But this urn holds the ashes of nearly one hundred generations of my ancestors, going back almost two thousand years."

"I understand why your grandmother won't leave without it," he said as she slowed the boat.

"According to GPS, this is close to the temple."

"And in the restricted area," he said.

"Ready?" she asked.

He nodded and pulled on his mask. A second later, they both flipped backwards off the edge of the boat and slipped into the cold, clear water.

At the same moment, a boat roared out of a nearby cove and headed toward their now empty craft.

Chapter Sixty-Eight

Wen saw the bubbles and churning motor of the approaching boat. They were all but defenseless underwater. She had to hope it was just tourists. As Wen signaled Chase to look up at the boat, now floating next to theirs, she knew trouble had arrived.

With hand signals, Chase asked if they should surface, but Wen shook her head and pointed down. There was a mission to complete. *Get the ashes, and then fight the battle,* she thought.

Then they saw it.

Like floating into an alien world, a city opened beneath them. In every direction they could see ornate buildings carved from stone, wide streets, and narrow alleys, as if they were flying over a city lost in time.

In spite of the looming danger above, and everything they had been through, she was awestruck and overcome by emotions at seeing her family's ancestral home just as it appeared when her grandmother was a girl.

Chase waved his arms. Wen followed his pointing hand,

and saw the temple. They swam down toward it. She looked back over her shoulder, the boats no longer in view, and so far no divers pursuing them. *Why would they come?* she wondered. *Whoever is up there knows we have limited air and will have to eventually return to the boat, where they'll be waiting.*

The temple appeared to have once had large double doors made of thick wood, but those were long gone, allowing them to swim right into the structure, which was also roofless. However, their quest was in the lower level, in a special room her grandmother had told them about.

Wen felt a surge inside her as soon as they navigated through the small front rooms and narrow halls and found the steps down. The layout was just as Zǔ mǔ had said. She could have cried when she saw the urn in the shape of a long narrow bell, carved with symbols and pictures that told the story of her family's beginning. Even in the murk, it seemed to glow as soon as she shined her light on it. Chase came in behind her and found himself spellbound, having the very real sense of being the first explorers to uncover an ancient Egyptian tomb.

Yet there wasn't time to marvel. Wen took out the dive bag they had purchased, large enough and strong enough to carry the heavy urn. She had originally planned to simply carry the bag, but now with a pending battle awaiting them, she found a way to strap it to her air tank.

Chase had a speargun, but otherwise they would face whatever awaited without weapons.

Surprisingly, the battle began as soon as they cleared the Temple. What Wen first believed to be underwater mines fell around them. They easily dodged what turned out to be basketball-sized rocks, but that was only the initial volley. As they swam on, gallon size containers rained down and began exploding.

Every communication had to be through hand signals and visuals between them, but the depth charges clouded the once clear waters and Wen lost sight of Chase. The next bomb detonated a few feet from Wen and blew her back into the murky depths. In a disoriented daze, she swam in the wrong direction for almost thirty seconds, winding up deeper and farther away from the boat. Wen found herself in a different part of the city, in a large, cavernous building that may have been a trading center. Finally, she righted herself and swam up fast until the water was clear again.

Chase, not seeing Wen, decided he had to get to the surface and try to take out whoever was attacking. Suddenly, harpoons zinged in around him, one bounced off his air tank. He knew there was one chance to neutralize the enemy; a single spear in his gun.

What if there's more than one? he wondered. *There might be ten.*

Capsize the boat, that's my only hope.

Chase surfaced and saw a wiry old man with long pants and no shirt stooped over the edge of a small boat, firing his spear gun into the water. He hadn't seen Chase. Chase looked around to see if Wen had come up yet, but didn't see her anywhere, so he aimed and fired his spear at the man. The spear stuck into the side of the boat at least a foot from his target. The man turned and aimed at Chase, but just before he pulled the trigger, he fell backwards into the water.

At least Chase *thought* he'd fallen out of the boat, until he saw Wen fighting with the man. The two were splashing and swinging, but Wen had a disadvantage, weighed down by the tank and urn. Chase swam toward them. By the time he reached them, Wen had the man in a choke hold.

"Who are you? Who sent you?" she screamed at him, gasping for air.

"I protect the city, you are robbers, I protect the city," he kept repeating.

"We are not robbers!"

"Liar, you take things!"

"This belongs to my family."

"What family?"

"Sung, this belongs to the Sung's."

"You are Sung?" he asked, his voice less hostile.

"I am Sung," she said, releasing him. "I am Sung."

He asked her which Sung still lived nearby, and Wen told him her grandmother's name.

"I am Pángxiè," he said. "I belong to the Deng family. Sung and Deng are friends many year." He smiled a toothless grin.

Chase unstrapped the urn from her back and lifted it into their boat. They both took off their air tanks and climbed aboard.

"I'm sorry Sung, very sorry. I protect the city under the lake. The city is not lost. It is still there."

They left Pángxiè babbling about the lake and the city. Later, Zǔ mǔ would send word that Pángxiè could have her house—it was much nicer than the shack he lived in—as long as he took care of the gardens.

After returning the boat and the gear, Wen presented the urn to her grandmother. Zǔ mǔ wept. She had not seen the sacred artifact in more than sixty years. Zǔ mǔ had two steaming bowls of soup and noodles for them, which she said contained healing medicinal herbs, and already had one suitcase packed. Wen gave her only ten minutes of peace before insisting they leave. She did not look back. It would have been too hard, she told them.

Mei Lein had arranged for them to stay in a safe house until WOLF operatives could get them out of the country that night. Along the way, her grandmother insisted on one last concession. They left Zǔ mǔ and the urn at a Buddhist temple, where she could meet with a monk, who had been a long time spiritual advisor to her. Just to be safe, they left the hard drive with her as well. The plan was for Chase, Wen, and Tu to wait at the safe house until two WOLF operatives showed up, then they would return to the monastery to get Zǔ mǔ on their way to the coast, where a boat would smuggle them all to South Korea. They expected to be in international waters in less than six hours.

None of them could have known that none of that was going to happen.

Chapter Sixty-Nine

Li's death squad was the best the MSS had—elite fighters trained in every aspect of weapons and surveillance—but in this case, the lethal members of the prestigious unit had been instructed *not* to execute their targets. It was a rare assignment that these militants were deployed for anything other than an assassination, and in this case it was critical they return three *live* bodies to the minister—an American man, a Chinese woman, and a Chinese boy.

They had been cautioned that the people were elusive and, particularly the woman, had been trained in MSS tactics, counter measures, and maneuvers. There were twelve members of the death squad, and Li was confident they would succeed in their mission if only he could discover their whereabouts. With hundreds of millions of cameras, and satellite surveillance, that shouldn't be a problem—particularly now that the pair were moving with a child. It was definitely a miscalculation on their part, one he still couldn't quite figure out.

The death squad found Chase and Wen at a WOLF safe

house after MSS computers matched coordinates and triangulated data pointing to a small town outside Hangzhou. The real break came once they figured out they could discard most of the bogus sightings of Chase and the woman that didn't include a boy.

They silently surrounded the house after satellite imaging showed the three fugitives going inside. Li watched from the command center, still nervous that the photos were only stills and were timed on seventy-five second intervals. The technician had assured him their degree of confidence was high.

"Between images 8487 and 8488, you can see them entering the dwelling," the tech said.

"It was a suspicious house," an analyst interjected. "AI review over previous imaging showed minimal use, and it was quickly suspected that this was a safe house or a meeting place for dissidents."

"Structure is quiet," an agent on the scene informed them over a crackling communications link. "One light is on. All shades drawn."

The twelve member team surrounded and waited for the order. They would not fail. Every entrance and every window was covered.

"Go ready?" Li asked. The question was relayed.

"Go ready," came the response.

"Go," Li proclaimed.

"Go! Go! Go!"

The front door was blown. Agents, wearing helmet cams and night vision, funneled into the small home. Li watched as the cameras caught all the action in their eerie green hue.

But as each room came up clear, the Minister assumed the inevitable—Malone had eluded them again. Yet, this time, they were only minutes behind them; the satellite imaging was only twelve minutes old.

"They can't be far," the agent in the house said through the com-link, as if echoing the Minister's thoughts.

"Take the neighboring houses," Li ordered. However, in the densely packed neighborhood, it would stretch their resources. There were houses on either side, another behind, and one across the narrow street. The MSS computers quickly calculated that in seventy-five seconds, the three fugitives could have gotten to any of the four houses. The commander on the ground ordered the death squad to break into four three-man teams and go simultaneously to every house, otherwise the variables changed, and an escape would be possible.

Wen knew about the intervals of the satellite photos, and she knew about the death squad. She figured that Li would decide not to have them executed, but it was likely that given the choice between letting them escape and killing them, the death squad would revert to their training and do the latter.

She counted seconds, and the three of them fled out the same door they went in as soon as the images reset. Only because Wen knew calibration codes had she been able to calculate when to start counting. Still, she'd been nervous that there'd been changes, or she'd be off. Yet as soon as they saw the death squad head for the safe house, they knew there was a chance to escape. Chase had been the last one through the door of the neighboring house with barely two seconds to spare.

Fortunately, they'd been able to pick up a small stash of WOLF weapons, but she knew there wasn't enough ammo for a prolonged battle. They'd have to take guns off dead MSS agents, and to do that . . .

Even if Wen had been alone, the odds were slim, but with Chase and Tu, everything took longer. Having a child in tow meant it was more likely they were going to get caught or killed. She imagined the Astronaut calculating their new odds of not making it out of China alive.

But Tu was part of the mission, and, more important, he was a little boy that didn't deserve the life he had. She had tried to imagine his future, but all those thoughts would have to be put on hold as she watched out the narrow window and waited for the attack she knew would come.

Wen started counting again. Three agents, split from the death squad, were going to hit the door of the house where they were hiding in twelve, ten . . .

Tu was under a table, Chase halfway up the stairs, just out of sight. Wen hid by the door. Hopefully, if all went well, the three killers would never reach Chase or the boy.

Eight seconds.

Wen, already thinking ahead, knew that after she took out these three, there would be three more, and three more again, and then, if she got the last three, their lead would have evaporated to nothing.

Six seconds.

She imagined the attack as if she were one of the death squad on the other side of the door. The MSS training, every move, every tactic, had been hammered into those elite operatives. She knew where their eyes would go, how their arms would swing, the position and angles of the guns, when the triggers would be pulled.

Four seconds.

Wen glanced up the stairs and frowned when she saw just the shadow of a hand. The agents would see it, too. It was too late to tell Chase to move six inches further up the stairs, but maybe she could use his error to her advantage.

Two seconds.

If the first agent saw the shadow he would think two things: one, they've got the right house, and two, that's where Wen was waiting, because she never would have been behind the door. They would know . . . but she knew something they didn't.

Chapter Seventy

The front door blew open, barely staying on its hinges, and swung hard, hitting a narrow marble table that prevented it from smashing into the wall. The storming MSS agents were too concerned with the stairs and the hallways to realize Wen was in the cavity behind the door. By the time the third man did cleanup, it would be too late.

She dropped the first two with clean single shots to the head. The third went for her, but he'd forgotten about the shadow. Chase put three bullets into his spinal cord, and he never moved again.

"The gunfire is going to bring the other agents!" Wen yelled.

"Let's get out of here!"

"No time," she said, picking up MSS guns and ammo while moving into the kitchen. "I've got a second plan."

Tu was quickly moved to the cupboards under the sink. Wen deftly got herself concealed on top of the kitchen cabinet—a narrow space barely large enough to hold her.

Chase would be the most exposed, as he would be in the half-bath off the kitchen.

"Use the mirror to determine when to shoot," she instructed him.

This time, her counting was only an estimate. Twenty seconds, she guessed. It took them twenty-three. Two agents entered the open front door. A third forced through the kitchen door. This had been her worst-case scenario, one she knew could happen, but preferred it did not. Wen had no choice but to take out the kitchen agent, thereby revealing her hiding place.

The other two moved quickly but cautiously down the hall. Chase got the first one in the leg while Wen sprang off the top of the cabinets, finished the first one, and engaged in a firefight with the second agent. She had to prevent a drawn-out gun battle that would give the other agents more time to get there. She knew the only way to avoid that was to run. She screamed in Mandarin for them to run, and then knowing that only Tu could understand the command, she added in Dutch, a language the MSS did not teach its officers, for him to stay right where he was.

The final agent, believing she was fleeing, ran after her, but knowing someone was in the half-bath, he stopped there and began firing into the small space.

After estimating his arrival time, Wen returned at the same instant and shot the man from the kitchen. "That's six down, six to go," Wen said as she pulled Tu from under the sink. She covered his eyes, told him to get on her back and hold on, and, carrying him, ran past all the dead agents and headed upstairs. His lungs betrayed him while he held onto her neck as she took two steps at a time.

"What's wrong?" she asked, hearing his asthmatic breathing.

"It's okay, Zǔ mǔ gave me magic paste—mud and plants," he said shoving the herbs in his nose, calming his breathing almost instantly.

Wen said a silent thank you to her grandmother.

"You didn't tell me I was going to be the decoy again," Chase said as he followed her.

"It should go without saying."

"Do we really want to be upstairs?"

"It's not my favorite place to defend, but this time the final six will come at once."

"Our only escape is through them," Chase said.

"That's right. I'm sure they've given up on taking us alive."

"I want to go home," Tu said.

"I'm sorry, honey," Wen said, pushing him into a closet. "We're almost through this. Just be quiet, and we'll get you out of here. Not a sound, okay?"

He nodded, tears filling his eyes and staining his cheeks. She closed the door.

"Top of the stairs," Wen told Chase. "Easiest place to defend."

"I think I'd rather be a decoy," he muttered, knowing the agents would charge up the stairs.

Wen started checking the windows, certain that's where the death squad would be coming from.

Before Wen could start counting again, it began. Forty-eight seconds later, Chase had killed three agents. Wen had killed one, and Tu was gone.

Chapter Seventy-One

Wen looked in the closet and couldn't believe her mistake. "The attic access is in here!"

"The last two agents must have come in and scooped him up," Chase said.

"Where did they go?"

Chase climbed up into the attic. Wen ran down the stairs.

One of the agents Chase shot on the steps, a woman, grabbed Wen as she raced by and sent her tumbling down to the bottom.

Chase spotted Tu being carried along by the two surviving death squad agents. Being members of that elite unit meant they were two of the deadliest in all of the MSS. He knew if he didn't rescue Tu now, he'd never see him again. Tu would be killed, or put into a place far worse then they'd gotten him from.

As he ran full stride across the roof and jumped down to the top of a lower garage, the bleak scenarios played out in his mind. Now that the MSS knew about the experiments on the children, they would destroy the evidence. He wondered if the girls were already dead.

He *had* to get Tu. He felt like a father, as if superpowers had electrified his legs. He had never felt so determined and lethal.

Chase only had a vague idea where they were headed, but as he came off the garage and landed in weedy grass, he was closer to them than expected. Chase saw Tu's terror stricken face being carried by a killer. Their eyes met, and somehow, although still hours new to the great big world, Tu seemed to know instinctively not to yell, or plead for Chase to save him.

However, at the same moment, one of the men turned and spotted Chase, who dove for cover, knowing the bullets would be there before he could get clear. A second later, bullets tore up the ground. Chase rolled next to a car for cover. At the same time, the residents, who'd just arrived home, ran behind their house.

Chase didn't understand why they were taking the boy and leaving him, until he realized that the boy was bait. They were luring him out of the house so he could be arrested or killed. The last two agents were smart enough to know the house was a death trap.

"Where's Wen?" he muttered, crawling toward another house, which would get him closer to the agents while also blocking their view of him. He'd seen a modest ornamental brick pattern on the corner which would allow him to quickly climb up to the roof. Even before he completed the thought, he was pulling himself above the rain gutter. Chase dashed up to the peak and down the other side, caught sight of his target, and leapt only a breath after he'd spotted the agent carrying Tu. By the time he landed on the agent, he had his gun arranged to smash the man in the head as they went down. Fortunately, the agent broke his fall.

"Run, Tu!" Chase yelled.

Tu was already running, having no idea where he was going, just trying to get away from the bad man.

Chase kept the momentum that had carried him to the ground and came up firing. The last agent was momentarily torn between chasing the kid, or shooting Chase.

In his panic, Tu made a costly mistake and ran back toward Chase. Now the agent could kill them both in one sweep. Chase fired toward the man, who had a large tree for cover, then tackled Tu. He brought the boy down, covering him with his body, trying to shield him from the shots. In the subsequent echoing of gunfire, Chase wondered how he wasn't dead, but as he turned to look, he saw the reason why.

Wen had killed the last agent. She was bleeding. Before he could reach her, she collapsed to the ground.

Chapter Seventy-Two

The president had declared martial law in parts of the country and more than ten thousand had been arrested. WOLF's entire presence in China had been apprehended, including Mei Lein and the men who were to smuggle Chase, Wen, Zǔ mǔ, and Tu out of the country. Military checkpoints were going up everywhere as China restricted the movements of Westerners throughout the country. The mass surveillance super state was closing in.

Chase ran to Wen. The blood didn't all belong to her, but enough of it told him she'd been shot or stabbed. He couldn't tell which. When he moved her arm, she came to with a painful cry.

"Your arm is broken," he said. "Where were you shot?"

"Not shot, stabbed," she said woozily.

"We can't stay. Can you walk?"

"Yes," she said, but collapsed again as she tried to stand.

Chase picked her up, careful to avoid her arm. "Tu, you'll need to walk. Stay right next to me."

"I want to go back!" Tu cried. "Please, Chase Bank, take me back to my sisters!"

"I'm sorry, Tu, we can't go back there right now. The same bad men are waiting there."

"Are they hurting my sisters?" His voice was filled with terror.

"No, they won't hurt your sisters, but we can't go back there."

"Then where will we go?"

Chase was used to thinking of Tu as a super bright individual, and yet looking at him, he saw a scared little boy who had never been away from home before. He tried to reassure him with his eyes. Chase could do that, as a man of the world, somebody who had survived more than his share of situations just like this. Chase relayed all the confidence that came with being Chase Malone, and Tu seem to respond. His expression calmed, just a little.

"We help Wen now," Tu said, trying to sound brave.

They hurried over to the MSS vehicles. Chase got one started. Wen crawled under the dashboard in the passenger seat.

"What are you doing?" Chase asked, concerned she was in more pain.

"MSS has tracking chips in all their vehicles. I'm disabling it," Wen said.

"How bad are your injuries?" Chase immediately regretted asking the question in front of Tu.

"I'm fine, but we have to go now," Wen said, her answer assuring Tu while she admonished Chase with her eyes.

"We're going to be okay," Chase said to Tu, who seemed mesmerized as they got onto a busy street.

Chase tried calling Mei Lein, but she didn't answer. Jo and Angúo were dead. They only had three other numbers, and none of them went through.

Wen somehow maintained consciousness, but at moments closed her eyes. The rest of the time she watched the sky, the road, the trees, seemingly trying to peer into invisible dimensions. Her concentration was intense, as she tried to recall every piece of training she had received, every MSS tactic, looking for an edge, a way out.

Tu finally broke from his spell of the busy world and looked at Wen with confused eyes, asking in a rapid, panicked voice, "Why are all these guns necessary? Who is trying to hurt us? Is this my fault for leaving Jang House?"

"No, these bad people were coming anyway," Wen said to him. "You've done nothing wrong."

Then they saw the checkpoint up ahead.

Chase turned off before the checkpoint, hoping they didn't arouse suspicion from the busy soldiers. Wen dialed the Astronaut. "We have the boy, we have the drive, but we have no way out."

"You have awakened the sleeping dragon," the Astronaut said. "The government is acting as if they are at war. Thousands of dissidents have been rounded up. International airports are armed camps—"

"Can you get us out?"

"No, but I know someone who can."

Wen knew he meant Tess, and told him the location of the Monastery. He promised to call them back.

Two miles from the Monastery, there was another checkpoint. This time there was no way around it. Chase pulled into the trees and they went on foot. Wen could only make it short distances before needing to be carried again, as she continued to lose blood. In all the things they'd been through together, for the first time, Chase was afraid Wen was going to die.

Chapter Seventy-Three

Tess, still watching the crisis in China with increasing alarm, accepted a call in Mission Control from the one person who could reach her anywhere.

"Well, Nash Graham, how nice to hear from you," she said to the Astronaut, signaling to her technicians to try to locate the source of the call even though she knew it would almost certainly be a waste of time.

"You must know why I'm calling."

"Because you're ready to come back to work for CISS?"

"No. You need to get them out."

"Who?"

"Tess."

"I would love to help them, but China is out of control right now, and you know what the leaders there do when things get out of hand. They kill people. *Lots* of people. It's too messy."

"You need to get them out," he repeated.

"Too risky. International incident all over this one. A serious one. Prelude to *war* serious."

"You need to get them *now*."

"Maybe we can figure something out as a favor to you—but only if you come back to work for us."

"You already have three Astronauts."

"One can never have too many. Besides, you're the best."

"You'll rescue them even without my agreement. If they get caught . . . "

"It's just too risky to get them."

"Too risky not to."

"Join us Nash, or they stay in China."

"Get them out right now, or I'll offer the MSS my services."

"My oh my . . . I don't see what Wen sees in you. All that anger pent up inside you."

"Only you bring it out."

She smiled, taking that as a compliment. "Where are they? We seem to have misplaced them."

Minutes after they arrived at the Monastery, a flying saucer shaped stealth-coated attack helicopter landed in the compound. It had been borrowed from HITE after Gatewood authorized the mission. The futuristic chopper had been deployed by a big altitude military transport plane which had been positioned for just such an evacuation. A medic was on board to attend to Wen's injuries. The flight in and out was invisible, thanks to another HITE technology—digital cloaking. The risks were enormous in utilizing such weaponry in Chinese airspace and territory, but the very nature of the advanced systems meant it was likely they would never know, and even if they guessed, it would be impossible to prove a thing.

As soon as the pilot announced they were in international air space, Wen decided it might be possible to trust Tess a little. Zǔ mǔ had never been on a plane before, and felt sick. However, Tu was very excited, especially when Chase told him he was going to the mythical land called America, where he would get to meet the Astronaut.

Epilogue

Li was demoted within hours of Chase and Wen escaping the country. His new position, both punishment and warning, was to run China's largest and most secret prison camp—the brutal Lingchi Prison. Those who knew about it said, "If you go in, you never come out." The name, roughly translated, means a slow, lingering death, or death by one thousand cuts. The isolated labor camp, located in the far western region of the country, had been operated by the MSS for more than two decades—although the government steadfastly denied its existence. Lingchi was as close to a cold, bitter hell as there was on earth.

Shen managed to avoid a sentence to Lingchi by cleverly covering his tracks. However, the new MSS minister quickly demoted him to a non-important regional post. Tess believed they now had an asset inside the MSS, that Shen would act as a CISS mole, but he thought differently, that he'd gotten away with it, that there was no way to prove he'd helped her. Their dual would flare up in the future, but for now, Tess was willing to let things settle down.

Under an alias, Chase leased a nice home on ten acres in a San Jose, California suburb, for Zǔ mǔ and Tu. The area had a large Asian population, so they would blend in. He also hired one of the most elite security firms in the world to protect the property in case the MSS ever managed to track them. The plan was to move them often, with Wen's grandmother homeschooling the boy, or the other way around. Wen was also working on a plan to allow Tu to be able to make and play with friends his own age.

HITE got to keep the drive with all the Ming Rénshēng data. Holt Gatewood believed his agency should get the boy as well. However, for now, Chase and Wen were winning that fight.

"Just get him to eighteen," Wen said. "The main thing is to keep his identity secret."

"We're good at that," Chase said. "And hiding. If anyone comes for him, we've got an escape plan."

The US had convened closed-door meetings at the United Nations and presented evidence of Ming Rénshēng to enough other nations that a unified world front against China's gene editing ambitions had begun. It was too soon to tell how effective it would be, but key leaders across the globe were intent on stopping the Chinese, while hopeful a war over the issue could be averted.

The MSS still hadn't identified Wen, but the new Minister had made it a priority. Chase and Wen believed it was only a matter of time before they unraveled her past.

"Then what?" Wen asked, as she and Chase watched Tu planting a garden with Zǔ mǔ.

Wen's grandmother looked up to Wen and shouted, "Tu remembers everything, every herb and plant I taught him in China. He's found all the similar ones here. He is amazing!"

She smiled so wide, Wen felt, for once, how right it was to bring them here.

Chase worried about Tu's safety, thinking back on the last attempt of the mysterious shadow people to kill them when they were backpacking out of the Marble Mountains in California. They were no closer to figuring out who those pursuers were. The unanswered question of the shadow people's identity drove Wen crazy, and now the MSS could also be coming for them.

"If the MSS," Wen began, "what if—"

"We're running anyway," Chase said, putting his arm around her. "Does it really matter how many are chasing us?"

Next in the Chase Malone Thriller series

vinci-books.com/chasing-kill

The plan: take down the world's digital backbone.

When a sinister plot emerges to bring modern life to its knees, a brilliant billionaire and a lethal ex-agent are all that stand between civilization and chaos.

Turn the page for a free preview…

Chasing Kill: Chapter One

Watching a man who would never again know freedom, who'd been in hiding far longer and under greater fear than himself, Chase Malone felt suddenly frightened.

"The world has turned upside down," he said, thinking about his own time on the run, now spanning nearly two years.

Wen, his partner, and a former spy, met his eyes. She, too, had been staring intently as the man walked away, weaving in and out of the pedestrian crowds. "Isn't that what we're trying to fix?"

"I'm not sure we can ever win," he replied, as they stood on a busy street in Moscow on a warm afternoon. "Do you think they'll get him?"

"Sooner or later," Wen said sadly. "I'm surprised he's lived this long."

As so often happened between Chase and Wen, their thoughts mirrored each other's. Wen had become a fugitive before Chase, and was a large part of the reason he was no longer a free man. Yet standing in that constrained city, its breeze scented with arugula and beef, both were grateful for what they had—so much more freedom than the man who'd just left them, a person whom many hailed as a hero, and others deemed a villain.

"He's a man without a country," Chase said, his gaze still following the person they'd just spent forty-five minutes with. "It's ironic that we would ask for his assistance."

"He gave up his freedom for many of the same reasons we did," Wen said.

"Do you think he'll help us?"

"He's a cautious man, but as soon as he verifies that we're not one of his enemies, he will." Wen, trained in psychology, had an uncanny ability to read people. It had saved their lives countless times. Of course, her training in all aspects of espionage, weapons, and martial arts, had also gotten them through many more horrendous situations.

They could still see him, and thought it curious that he'd never once turned back to so much as glance at them. "He must trust us. Five hundred feet away and he hasn't looked over his shoulder." Chase's blue eyes squinted, trying not to miss anything, while he rubbed at an old injury on his arm.

"No, he has somebody watching us." Wen scanned the crowd, as she'd been doing since before the man had arrived. "He has limited resources . . . probably aren't many people on his team . . . certainly one . . . maybe as many as three." She'd identified two suspects already. "We've been under surveillance the whole time. They're still out there."

"Which ones?" Chase asked.

Without looking directly at them, Wen described their appearances and locations. "They're good. I can almost always ID the watch, but these are very, *very* good."

Wen had taught Chase many things since she'd come back into his life two years earlier, yet he still couldn't flush out the pros. Even with all the people constantly after them, it remained difficult for him. Many pursuers they'd identified, others they simply called "the shadow people"—a mysterious group who'd been trailing them relentlessly for unknown reasons.

Chase's life as a billionaire engineer in Silicon Valley seemed far away and long ago. But as he watched the man turn a corner and finally disappear, he couldn't help but wonder about the infamous person with whom they'd just met.

As difficult as it is for me to get some decent sleep, for Edward Snowden, it must be next to impossible.

"There!" Wen whispered urgently.

"One of Snowden's people?" Chase asked, not sure why there was so much alarm in her voice.

"No. Someone else. Someone coming for *us*!" The ex-Chinese agent's lithe body whipped around after giving Chase the 'go now' eye.

Chase instinctively thought of the shadow people, and began to run.

Chasing Kill: Chapter Two

Chase followed Wen into a narrow alley between two buildings older than his country of birth. He knew she'd already figured out where to run. Wen always had a plan. Immediately upon walking on a new street, entering a building, a room, anywhere, Wen assessed the best escape route, strategic places to fight, every angle of pursuit, and hundreds of other variables mere mortals would never consider.

Her training and experience allowed her to create a strategy out of thin air. However, in this case, she'd had lots of time to plan. Snowden and Wen had chosen the location because of its openness, abundance of exit points, and public crowds that would make an ambush—even in a professional hit—difficult.

They rounded a corner. "Another!" Wen said breathlessly.

Chase saw a second man approaching and realized they were in real trouble. He followed automatically as Wen darted into a building.

The bustling streets and city noises evaporated. They were suddenly in a colorful wonderland of toys and brightly painted wooden Russian Matryoshka nesting dolls of every size—some taller than Chase himself. Their presence caused an immediate disruption as they burst into the store among only a small handful of customers.

"We've lost our young son," Wen called out in perfect Russian. "Have you seen him?" She held out her hand to indicate a child no more than three feet tall.

The shopkeeper, a round, gray lady, gave an immediate look of concern, but shook her head. "*Nyet.*"

"Is there a back door?" Chase blurted out in English.

Wen repeated the question in Russian.

The shopkeeper lit up and pointed to the rear of the store, seemingly happy to be able to give them a positive response. Wen and Chase had never stopped moving, because even if there had not been another exit, they would've had to get as far inside the building as possible before the fight began. Chase pushed through the heavy wooden door, ejecting them out onto a winding side street.

"Listen," Wen said, commotion erupting from the toy shop behind them. "At least one of them is close."

"We're going to have to confront them at some point," Chase yelled, looking for a good place to hide as they sprinted past dumpsters, empty pallets, and discarded barrels.

"We're in *Moscow*. This is not a good place for a fight. We don't need any extra attention."

"I know, but—"

"It will do us no good to defeat the shadow people, only to get taken into custody by the Russian FSB. This is one time where escape is the only way we can win."

"How many are there?"

"I saw two. That means four."

Chase wasn't going to ask *how* she knew that. He'd learned that she always knew. "Then our best way to escape is to cut down their numbers," he said, pointing to a cut out in the curve that held two dumpsters.

Wen nodded reluctantly, knowing what he was thinking.

As the two of them wedged themselves together in the tight space, Chase realized the odds were they would never get off the street alive.

Grab your copy…
vinci-books.com/chasing-kill

About the Author

USA TODAY Bestselling Author Brandt Legg uses his unusual real life experiences to create page-turning novels. He's traveled with CIA agents, dined with senators and congressmen, mingled with astronauts, chatted with governors and presidential candidates, had a private conversation with a Secretary of Defense he still doesn't like to talk about, hung out with Oscar and Grammy winners, had drinks at the State Department, been pursued by tabloid reporters, and spent a birthday at the White House by invitation from the President of the United States.

At age eight, Legg's father died suddenly, plunging his family into poverty. Two years later, while suffering from crippling migraines, he started in business, and turned a hobby into a multi-million-dollar empire. National media dubbed him the "Teen Tycoon," and by the mid-eighties, Legg was one of the top young entrepreneurs in America, appearing as high as number twenty-four on the list (when Steve Jobs was #1, Bill Gates #4, and Michael Dell #6). Legg still jokes that he should have gone into computers.

By his twenties, after years of buying and selling businesses, leveraging, and risk-taking, the high-flying Legg became ensnarled in the financial whirlwind of the junk bond eighties. The stock market crashed and a firestorm of trouble came down. The Teen Tycoon racked up more than a million dollars in legal fees, was betrayed by those closest to him, lost his entire fortune, and ended up serving time for financial improprieties.

After a year, Legg emerged from federal prison, chastened and wiser, and began anew. More than twenty-five years later, he's now using all that hard-earned firsthand knowledge of conspiracies, corruption and high finance to weave his tales. Legg's books pulse with authenticity.

His series have excited nearly a million readers around the world. Although he refused an offer to make a television movie about his life as a teenage millionaire, his autobiography is in the works. There has also been interest from Hollywood to turn his thrillers into films. With any luck, one day you'll see your favorite characters on screen.

He lives in the Pacific Northwest, with his wife and son, writing full time, in several genres, containing the common themes of adventure, conspiracy, and thrillers. Of all his pursuits, being an author and crafting plots for novels is his favorite.

Acknowledgments

Like Chasing Dirt, Chasing Life was written entirely in the wilds of Oregon and California. It was edited and revised at my desk, and both parts of the process were really fun.

As always, my first two readers deserve the first and most thanks—

Roanne, my wife, and Barbara Blair, my mother, waded through the early drafts and made crucial suggestions and corrections.

To my four brothers, who are each inspirations and good friends in their own ways.

Again, Jack Llartin did the final read, diligently hunting down all the typos and things that we missed.

Big gratitude to Melanie C. Hansen, who miraculously came in and found two handfuls of typos that got missed on an earlier book, and has been helping out ever since. She's especially good at tracking down the elusive Sigosaur.

And, finally, to Teakki, who patiently waited to watch monster movies until I finished writing each day. Monster movies!?

And to you, for turning these pages. You have made my dreams come true by making it possible for me to support my family by writing books. I'm grateful you found my work and took a chance on me. See you on the next adventure . .